ANOTHER CHANCE AT LOVE

G. FAY

Book Cover by: Carefree Consulting
Book Layout by: Opeyemi Ikuborije

Printed in the United States of America

ISBN: 979-8-9857654-0-3

CONTENTS

Acknowledgements

G. Fay expresses much love and heartfelt thanks to:

God, for being my rock and for giving me the strength to believe in myself. This journey has opened my eyes to believe in an accomplishment I never thought would come to fruition.

My mom, I will ALWAYS cherish you. My heart has not been the same since God called you home. I will forever treasure the love and support you gave me.

My husband, Matt, for your CONSTANT love, support, and encouragement. Life would not be the same without you.

My sweet daughter, Kalani Alicia, for always pushing me to never give up on my desire to write. Your support and encouragement mean more than you'll ever know. Your expertise and knowledge played a pivotal role in this endeavor.

My sisters and niece, Sadie (Bay) Johnson, for your support and enthusiasm, and for always making me laugh. Now, you can finally read it! Wenda Stuward and Sharde Malone, your support is greatly appreciated.

My grandson, Jameel, I hope this inspires you to one day be the best writer that you can be and to never give up on your dreams.

CHAPTER 1

The Wedding Day

Awakened by Bluebirds chirping outside her window. Jazmine turned over to gaze at her wedding dress, with pearls and lace, hanging on the outside of her closet door. *Wow, this is it, this is the big day.* She smiled but had mixed emotions about how her life might change. Noah had been acting strange and she had no idea why. Determined not to focus on her concerns about him, she put all her energy into celebrating her special day. The aroma of bacon and toast filled the air while she jumped out of bed. She threw water on her face, brushed her teeth, and got dressed for her morning jog when she heard a knock on her door.

"Yes?" she said.

"Hey sweetie, are you awake?" her mom asked.

"Good morning, Mom, yes I am. Come on in."

"Good morning, baby, I'm so excited for you. This is your big day. Everything is in order, so you have nothing to worry about."

"Oh, I'm not worried, Mom. I'm happy and just a little nervous, but I'm good. I'm going to go for a jog, so maybe that'll help to calm my nerves."

"I'm sure that'll help. I made breakfast if you want to grab a bite to eat before heading out. I bet Noah is excited and nervous too."

"Maybe so."

"Why do you say that?"

"Well, he's still working in DC and I'm not sure when he'll be coming back home to stay. He keeps saying he's working on a big project, which involves millions of dollars, so he can't leave yet. I don't like it, but I guess I'll just have to be patient. I'm sorry Mom, I shouldn't be telling you all of this on my wedding day. I don't want you to be thinking about any of that. I'm sure everything will work out."

"Yes, it will. But I don't want you trying to control everything on your own, Jazmine. So, if you need help or just want to talk about it, you know I'm here for you."

"I know Mom."

She took a couple of bites from a bagel with cream cheese and gave her mom a kiss.

"I'll be back shortly."

"Be careful out there. Do you have your taser on you?"

"Yes."

Jazmine hoped jogging would help to relieve her anxiety about marrying Noah. She'd just graduated from UC Berkeley with a degree in Education. One year prior, he'd taken a job as an Engineer at Genentech, in Washington, DC, and promised to return home when they got married. At first, they traveled back and forth to visit each other, but she became uncomfortable when he started spending more time in DC. She loved the crisp morning air against her skin, as jogging and watching the birds hover over Lake Merritt gave her a sense of peace. *This is so therapeutic.* Living in the bay area and being a part of all it had to offer, had captured her heart. Although Oakland, like most urban cities had its issues with crime, Jazmine had grown accustomed to being cautious with her surroundings while appreciating all the different cultures. A mixture of flavors from the restaurants as they started to prepare food for the day filled the air.

After her jog, her excitement and anticipation increased as time for the wedding approached. The weather had forecasted around eighty-degrees with a light breeze. Even though she never imagined it would happen, she always dreamed of getting married in an elegant outside setting. They agreed on having a small wedding, limited only to family and close friends. The wedding took place at 3:00 pm on Saturday, May 8th, 2021, in the Berkeley hills overlooking the bay area. The picturesque landscape provided a scenic display with plenty of shade trees. The wedding party included her sister, Jessica, as her maid of honor, and her two closest friends, Erica, and Sophia, as her bridesmaids.

Jazmine impressed everyone in her stunning custom-made wedding dress with her hair artfully braided in a chic updo. Ringlets hung down to adorn her face, and she wore a beaded hair piece, which complimented her hair. Her smooth chocolate skin and almond shaped eyes captivated Noah as he couldn't take his eyes off her. Their love and affection toward each other showed on their faces as they never stop smiling. Jazmine had fallen head over heels in love with Noah and she loved everything about him. He had a charming personality, a sexy smile, and his athletic build made it hard for her to resist him. He had spoiled her, and she loved it, but his love for her went beyond her ability to capture his attention. He admired her sensitivity and desire to help others in dealing with their problems. The next day they flew to Honolulu, Hawaii to celebrate their honeymoon for a week.

"You alright baby?" Noah asked. "I know you don't like flying but we'll be there soon."

"I'm good," she said, squeezing his hand. "I hate turbulence and I don't think I'll ever get used to this crap."

"Do you want something to drink to help you relax?"

"No, I'll be fine."

"Hello everyone, sorry for the bumpy ride," the pilot said. "Due to a storm, we hit a rough patch. But rest assured we'll be landing in beautiful Honolulu, in about twenty minutes, where the temperature is in the high eighties."

During their honeymoon, they had a great time swimming, snorkeling, and having romantic dinners by the ocean. She became uneasy, the closer it got to the end of their honeymoon because she'd been waiting for the right time to tell him about her new job, and to discuss when he'd be moving back to California. On their flight home, they held hands and talked about all the fun they had in Hawaii. When they arrived at his high-rise apartment, he reminded her he needed to return to work the next morning.

CHAPTER 2

After the Honeymoon

When Noah got home from work, Jazmine had surprised him by cooking his favorite meal. He'd stopped by the store and picked up a bottle of wine before heading home.

"Hey baby, how was your day?" she asked. "You look a little tired. Did you make any progress on the project?"

"Yes, it was a productive day, but we still have a long way to go. Come here, I missed you." He pulled her close to him and kissed her. "It sure smells good in here, what did you cook?"

"Rib eye steak with mash potatoes."

"Yum, rib eye steak. That sounds delicious. I'll take a quick shower and I'll be right back."

"Alright, I'll set the table."

Jazmine was eager to tell him about her new job offer and to discuss his return to California. After his shower he went back into the kitchen for dinner.

"You feel a little better now?" she asked.

"Yes, sometimes that job wears me out. It's not so much the work, it's my coworkers. At times they wait until the last minute to finish their part of the project, which slows down the progress of getting it completed. But I've been dealing with this since I started, so you'd think I'd be used to it by now. For the most part, I do enjoy my job though."

Jazmine couldn't care less about whether he enjoyed his job.

"I understand your frustration. And I'm glad you feel better. I've been slaving over that stove for hours, so let's eat."

He smiled. "Okay Jazz if you say so. It looks delicious."

"Thank you, baby. I hope you like it."

"Wow, this taste really good, Jazz. I need to hurry up and move back home if you're going to be cooking like this," he said, laughing.

After they cleaned up the kitchen, Jazmine was ready to discuss her concerns.

"Let's sit on the couch and have a glass of wine," she said.

"Okay, I'll get the bottle out of the fridge and grab a couple of glasses."

"I have something I want to talk with you about."

He filled their glasses with wine, and after taking a couple of sips, he'd gave her his undivided attention.

"Two weeks ago, I accepted a position at Saint Mary's High School as an English teacher. I didn't want to mention it to you earlier because we were about to get married and go on our honeymoon, so I wanted to wait until we got back home. Plus, even though I accepted the position, I really didn't know if I should've taken it. I wondered if I should just move to Washington DC with you until you're able to come back home. So, when are you moving back to California?" she asked.

He sat his glass on the table. "Wow, congratulations baby, that's great, I'm so proud of you. I'm a little surprised you're just now telling me this. I mean, why didn't you tell me this before? Are we keeping secrets now?"

"Oh, no, no, I just didn't want anything to spoil our honeymoon, and I wasn't sure how you'd take it. I was expecting to start in September, but during the interview, to my surprise, they asked if I could start in June to teach summer school. I was hesitant at first, but I accepted it because this'll give me a chance to get familiar with teaching before the regular season starts."

"Oh wow, so you'll be starting soon."

"Yeah, pretty soon now."

"So, when are you moving back to Cali? Your manager knows we got married, right?"

"Yes, of course, but we have another major project coming up, which involves a big financial gain for the company. So, I'll be moving back to California when it's completed. When you get home, you can find a nice place for us, while I wrap things up here."

"Uh, okay, sounds like a good idea."

She wasn't happy he'd no immediate plans to come home but held back her emotions. The rest of the week, she made the best of their time together and cooked delicious meals or made reservations for a romantic dinner. At the end of the week, she had to pack up and leave for California to prepare for her new job.

Sunday afternoon, Noah drove her to the Washington National Airport for her 2:00 pm flight. On the way to the airport, they were quieter than normal. When they approached the drop off point, tears filled both their eyes while he held her hand. He parked the car, then got out to get her luggage. They held each other and kissed while trying to control their emotions. She pulled out a couple of tissues to wipe their faces. She hadn't seen him that emotional in a long time, not since his father passed.

"Call me when your flight arrives in California," Noah said, while helping to check in her luggage.

"I will baby."

That week Jazmine found an apartment she loved and called Noah right away.

"Hey baby, what do you think about the pictures I sent? I really love it. It has a nice view overlooking the bay and it has three bedrooms, which means we can have a room for an office and one for guests."

"It looks nice. So, if you really want it, and it feels right, just get it."

"Okay, I'll put down the deposit right now, and I'll call you back this evening."

"Sounds good. And thanks Jazz for finding us a place to stay. I'm sorry I couldn't be there to help you."

The following weekend, Noah flew to California to help her with the move-in. Since they didn't have much furniture, they went out and purchased new bedroom, living room, and kitchen furniture. He'd only come for a couple of days, which increased her anxiety because she figured he wouldn't be there for the delivery date.

CHAPTER 3

Feeling Abandon

The next three weeks, Jazmine kept busy decorating their apartment. She purchased candles and colorful pillows for the couch and hung striking abstract pictures on the wall. She'd ordered a 17x24 portrait of them on their wedding day and displayed it in an elegant Vera Wang frame in their living room. She worked hard to give it a warm and cozy feel and loved how it came with all the amenities. They made sure to text each other daily and talked on the phone every night, which only made her more frustrated. Although it didn't seem to bother Noah as much, it gave her a sense that he'd abandoned her.

Friday night, she tried to entertain herself by eating popcorn and watching "Girls Trip" starring, Tiffany Haddish. Her eyes welled up with tears, while trying to deal with the challenge of keeping busy. *Does he even realize what this is doing to me? He promised after we got married, he'd move back right away. Now he's talking a different story.* When her phone rang, she ran to pick it up, and tried to hold back her emotions when his name appeared on the Caller ID.

"Hey Noah."

"Hey Jazz. How's my baby doing?"

"I'm hanging in there. How're you?"

"I'm doing fine, missing you. This new project involves a lot of demands, and it's causing me to work on most weekends. So, right now I can't come to Cali as often as I'd planned. But once this project is over, I'm outta here. I love you, Jazz."

His voice appeared tired yet soothing, which helped her to stay calm. She came close to crying but didn't want him to know how frustrated she'd become.

"I understand, and I miss you too. The decorating is coming along good, and I wish you were here to see it. Everything looks so nice. I think you'll like how it all came together."

"I'm sure I will. And I promise I'll be there soon."

Jazmine didn't want to accept how demanding his job had become. She grew tired of spending every day and night alone while he lived in another state. A month had passed, and they'd only been together one time since their honeymoon. She picked up the phone to called Erica for support.

"Hello?"

"Hey Erica, how're you?"

"I'm good Jazmine, how're you? And how is newlywed life treating you?"

"Girl, it's rough to say the least. Noah's still in DC, and he just started working on a new project. Bottom line is, I don't know when he's coming back home, and I'm getting really irritated. It's all so overwhelming."

"I didn't know he was still gone. I'm so sorry. I know it must be hard for you to deal with, especially being newlyweds."

"Exactly. Last night he said he'd be coming home for good when this project is completed, but I don't know if I believe him. He seems to be content with the way things are. We just don't seem to be on the same page anymore, and I hope I didn't make a mistake in marrying him. Sometimes he doesn't even return my calls until the next day. What's up with that?"

"Hmm...well, you have to hang in there, Jazz, even though it's hard. He'll be home soon."

"I sure hope so because I expect my husband to be here with me. Not off in another state somewhere doing who knows what."

"I hear you, but he's probably working a lot of over time. You know how these jobs can be and with him being an engineer, I'm sure it can be demanding. So, give him some time. It'll all work out."

"Yeah, I guess so. But nothing should come before me. Anyway, I ran into Marcus at Starbucks a couple of days ago. Do you remember him? He played on the basketball team in high school."

"Oh yeah, I remember him. He always seemed a little weird to me."

"Yeah, he was popular, but he didn't hang out too much, he was more on the quiet side. So, since we realized we worked near each other, he asked me out for lunch the next day. He seemed like a nice guy when we were in high school, so I agreed to have lunch with him, which turned out nice."

"That sounds good. Hanging out with an old friend can be fun."

"We actually had good conversation, but I noticed he was kind of vague in talking about his personal life. He also asked me out for dinner on Saturday night, if I wasn't busy."

"Uh, I don't think that's a good idea, Jazz. I know you're frustrated with Noah and all, but I just don't want you to get too involved with Marcus."

"Well, I told him Noah is working out of town but will be home soon. You're right though, what am I thinking. I'll text him to let him know that I'll be busy this weekend."

Erica recognized that Jazmine didn't say, she'd tell him it wouldn't be a good idea.

"Just be careful, Jazz. I don't want you to get yourself in a situation that would cause you any trouble."

"I hear you. And I understand where you're coming from. Thank you for listening to me, and I hope I didn't whine your ear off too much about my situation with Noah."

"Girl, that's what friends are for. You can call me anytime. Let's get together soon like we use to and laugh about the crazy times we use to have. It'll help to relieve some stress."

"Yes, those were fun times. Okay, I'll be in touch."

"Alright, remember, call me anytime you need to talk."

"I will and thanks again Erica. I'll talk with you later."

Erica became concerned about her because of the void she'd tried to fill from Noah being away.

CHAPTER 4

Filling a Void

Sunday morning, Jazmine attended service at First Baptist Church, where her, Erica and Sophia use to go together. After service, she'd gained strength from the preached message and songs from the choir. She rushed home to call Noah, but it went to voice mail.

"Hi baby, I was thinking about you and wanted to hear your voice. I just got back home from church, which was really good. Give me a call back. I miss you so much."

Three hours later, Noah returned her call.

"Hey Noah."

"Hi baby, I'm sorry I missed your call. I just got back from the office."

"It's fine. Wow, so you're working on Sunday's now. How's that going?"

"It's going okay. I'm just trying to stay on top of things. I really miss you and I can't wait to see you. I'm sorry, Jazz, but I won't be able to fly out this weekend. This project has been a real headache and I've been working overtime to get it completed."

"Wow, really, this is just not right Noah. It's been over a month, and you haven't even seen our new furniture." Tears filled her eyes as she became overwhelmed with emotion.

"You're right and I know you're disappointed, but I'll definitely fly out in a couple of weeks. I already told my boss I won't be available to work."

That night she tried to fall asleep but tossed and turned most of the night. Later in the week she followed up with Marcus by sending him a text message.

Jazmine: Hey Marcus, I'm sorry I didn't get back with you sooner. I've been busy with work.

Marcus: No worries, I figured you were busy.

Jazmine: Do you still want to get together for dinner this weekend?

Marcus: Yes, of course. Are you available on Friday night?

Jazmine: Yes, I am.

Marcus: Cool, can I pick you up or would you prefer to meet at my place? Does 6:00 work for you?

Jazmine: Yes, 6:00 is fine, I'll come to your place. What's your address?

Marcus: 2476 Elmwood Dr. Apt C.

Jazmine: Okay, I'll be there.

All day Friday, Jazmine struggled with the idea of going out to dinner with Marcus, but her anger towards Noah motivated her. Determined to have a good time, she held back her emotions while getting dressed. She wore her black wide leg pants and her yellow silk blouse that bow tied around her neck. When she parked her car in the driveway of his apartment building, she'd received a text message from Erica.

Erica: Hey Jazz, I'm just checking on you and hope you're doing Okay.

Jazmine: I'm doing good. Thanks Erica, for checking on me and for the much-needed prayers. I really appreciate it. I'll see you tomorrow morning at church.

Before getting out of the car, she reflected on how much she loved Noah and thought maybe she'd become too selfish. When she knocked on the door, Marcus answered, giving her a hug.

"Hey there, I'm glad you made it. Come on in and have a seat. I'll be ready in just a few minutes. Would you like something to drink?"

"No, thank you. I'm good."

Jazmine recalled him being a gentleman in high school, which made her more comfortable. Right away she recognized he'd decorated his apartment like a true bachelor. He had one picture on the wall and a huge flat screen TV sitting next to an entertainment center. He also had a large aquarium with colorful fish inside.

"I love your aquarium. It's really nice and the fish are beautiful," she said.

"Thank you, Jazmine. It's one of my favorite hobbies. I get a kick out of watching them move around so freely in the water. Sometimes they even fight, which is funny to see. Alright, we better get going."

Marcus had dressed in slacks, and a cardigan, with a black trench coat over one arm. His charm and handsomeness threw her off, but she refused to compliment him. She simply planned to fill the void of being alone every night by going out to have a little fun. They had a great time eating dinner at the Top of the Mark in San Francisco overlooking the city. The views were spectacular, and she appreciated the special attention he gave her, but she refused to show any excitement. After dinner, they drove to the AMC theater in Emeryville. Because of the cold breeze, he placed his coat over her shoulders while they walked toward the theater. Due to Covid-19, there were seating limitations, but since it was the last showing, they ended up being the only ones there. They ate popcorn and laughed while watching, "Jungle Cruise" starring, Dwayne Johnson. When they arrived back at his apartment parking lot, she made sure to end the evening with a short and sweet expression of gratitude.

"Thank you for dinner and the movie, I had a good time."

"I had a good time as well, and I hope we can do it again soon."

She didn't respond and proceeded to get out of his car, while he jumped out and hurried to open the door for her.

"Would you like to come in for a drink?"

"No thank you, not this time," she said, smiling.

He gave her a hug, then held the door as she got into her car. She smiled, and waved goodbye before driving off.

The following Sunday after church, she told Erica about her evening out with Marcus and stressed her disappointment in Noah's constant excuses for not coming home.

"I really enjoyed myself and I know he did too. Don't worry, nothing happened between us; he only gave me a hug when we said good night. I even told him about the situation with Noah and he was very understanding. He suggested getting together again soon, but I'll think about it."

"Yes, you have to be careful not to get yourself into a difficult situation, Erica said."

Erica didn't want to come across as being judgmental or trying to get in Jazmine's business, instead she asked to pray for her. Tears were streaming down her face when Erica ended her prayer.

"Thank you, Erica. I really needed that."

CHAPTER 5

A Date Gone Wrong

Jazmine understood, she had to cease going out with Marcus but loved the idea of someone showing her the kind of attention she needed from Noah. Later in the week she received a text message from Marcus.

Marcus: Hi Jazmine, hope you're doing well. I was wondering if you'd like to get together for dinner on Friday.

Jazmine: Yes, I'd love too. "I'd love too, really Jazmine?" she asked herself. "I probably should take that back."

Marcus: Good, do you want to meet at my place or a restaurant?

Jazmine: I prefer a restaurant.

Marcus: How about meeting at Skates in Berkeley at 6:30?

Jazmine: I'll be there.

On the way to the restaurant, her phone rung.

"Hey Marcus."

"Hey there, I was wondering if you didn't mind having chinese food at my place? I'm pretty exhausted from working hard today."

"I really prefer to meet at a restaurant. I don't think that's a good idea. We can just get together another time."

"Well, I'm just a little tired and thought it'd be easier for me to pick up something, and we can watch a movie on netflix."

"Hm, I understand if you're that tired... I guess I can come by for a little while."

Before heading over to his place, she drove back home to change into more comfortable clothes. When she arrived and parked her car, her hands were sweating, and her heart had started beating fast. After she rung his doorbell, she'd changed her mind and ran back to the elevator. When the door opened to get on, Marcus got off.

"Hey there, I left my phone in the car and went back to get it. We must've missed each other while I was going down the elevator."

"You know, I was thinking the same thing," she said, sighing. "Let me check my purse again to make sure I have mines. Oh, here it is."

"Good, let's head back to my apartment."

Jazmine had failed to figure a way out. Right away, he gave her a compliment and took her hand while they walked back to his apartment. She started to pull her hand away, then figured it'd only be for a short time. She'd dressed down and wore no jewelry to express she only wanted to establish a friendship. *Why is he complimenting me? My braids are pulled back in a ponytail, and I just have on sweats and tennis shoes.*

The table had been set with two candles and a bottle of Chardonnay. She gave a short compliment to avoid showing any enthusiasm about being there.

"Nice set up."

"Thank you, just thought I'd make it special, for a special lady."

During dinner, Jazmine laughed at his jokes and the crazy stories he shared about his childhood. He had a good sense of humor, which made her more at ease and helped her to relax. After dinner, she needed to freshen up, while he turned on the TV to search for a movie on Netflix.

"Can I use your bathroom?"

"Sure, it's down the hall, the first door on the left."

While in the bathroom, she found a bottle of Gin sitting on the counter next to a bottle of Prozac. *Who keeps alcohol in their bathroom with a prescription of Prozac?* He'd forgotten to put those items away prior to her arrival. She became uncomfortable as she walked back to the living room.

"Is everything okay?" he asked, with a strange expression on his face.

"Yes, I just needed to freshen up a bit."

He turned down the volume on the TV.

"Tell me a little more about you and the kind of work you do?" he said.

This is odd, I already told him I was a teacher the other day and we talked in depth about it during dinner. She sat in a chair across from him to avoid an intimate atmosphere.

"Sure, although I think I've already shared a lot about me, so first tell me more about you? How has life been treating you since we graduated from high school?"

He sighed and poured himself a glass of Crown Royal Whiskey.

"Honestly, things have been tough lately."

Jazmine sat silent, trying to figure out where the bottle of whiskey had come from. She had a glass of wine after dinner but hadn't notice a bottle of whiskey. She wanted to give him a chance to talk because he'd been vague in talking about his personal life. She handed him a tissue while tears filled his eyes.

"Thank you for spending time with me, I know you're married, and you probably shouldn't be here."

"It's alright, I didn't have any real plans this evening. Is there something I can help you with, or do you just want to talk about it?"

She'd studied psychology as a minor in college and considered using her skills to help him work through his issues.

"I fell on hard times and I'm just trying to get through this. I might share it with you one day," he said, turning the volume back up on the TV.

"It's okay."

Ten minutes later, he'd poured himself a second glass of whiskey. "How does it look like life has been treating me?" he said. His tone had changed, which made her even more uncomfortable.

"I don't mean to pry, I just thought since we haven't seen each other in years we'd catch each other up on our lives."

It's obvious you turned out to be a self-centered a-hole. What happened to the nice quiet guy from high school? Jazmine suspected he'd been dealing with deeper issues and because of his slurred speech, she figured he had more to drink than what she'd witnessed.

"Come and sit on the couch so we can be closer."

"Uh, it's getting late and I'm tired, so I think I better be going. Plus, I have a lot of assignments to grade, and I need to get up early in the morning."

She stood up and went into the kitchen to get her jacket.

"Why do you think I asked you to come to my place?"

"I just thought we're getting together to have dinner."

He grabbed the bottle of whiskey from the coffee table and poured himself another drink. When she reached for her jacket, she'd noticed her clutch purse no longer sat on the kitchen counter.

"Where's my purse?"

"I don't know." He laughed, then got up and stumbled over to her putting his hands on her shoulders. "I'm not ready for you to go yet, so have a seat."

She squinted her eyes and stared at him. "Take your hands off me. You've had too much to drink, so I'm leaving. What did you do with my purse?"

He removed his hands from her shoulders after giving her a slight shove backwards, causing her to stumble.

"What the *hell* is wrong with you?"

"I'm sorry, I didn't mean for that to happen. You must've missed your step."

"You pushed me. You knew exactly what you were doing."

"No, no I really didn't mean it that way. I was just trying to be funny. But you're right. I should've never put my hands on you."

He reached for her hand, but she pulled it back. His attitude had changed from a gentleman to a mean bitter person, and even though he'd made her uncomfortable, she had confidence in her karate skills to protect herself.

"Alright, I'll come clean with you. I got laid off a year ago and I'm looking for another job. I'm sorry I lied to you, but I was embarrassed when you started telling me how great your life has been. I feel like my life is spiraling out of control and I just need some help. Please, can you sit back down and stay a little while longer?"

"But you told me you work close to me."

"I know, I know. I just made that up," he said, sighing. "What was I going to say, I was an executive for a big corporation, but I was fired? Because of one mistake, just one mistake, they let me go."

"Let me ask you something. Are you taking Prozac? Because I saw it sitting on your bathroom counter."

"Yes, but that's only the half of it. When I lost my job and my family, I started drinking alcohol heavily."

Jazmine agreed to stay a while longer, at least until she figured out where he'd hidden her purse.

"I can see that my leaving bothers you, so I'll just stay a little longer." *Maybe I can use my psychology skills to help this fool.*

After a while, his eyes became droopy, and she remained quiet, pretending to be interested in the movie.

"I'm going to have just one more. Would you like a drink?"

"No, I don't drink whiskey and I don't want to drink and drive."

"Good...good idea."

When he leaned in to pour his drink, she discovered her purse under the pillow next to him. Five minutes later he'd fallen asleep. She took her time and pulled her purse from under the pillow, and tip-toed to the door, unlocked it, and ran to the elevator. Once she reached her car, she jumped in and sped off while breaking down in tears.

CHAPTER 6

A Surprise Visit

When Jazmine got home, she fell on her bed and cried until midnight. *Why did things turn out this way? I would've never been in that position if Noah would just come home.* The past couple of nights she'd been short when talking to Noah on the phone. Every Saturday morning, he called at 9:00 am, but not that morning. She picked up the phone to call him and left him a message.

"Hi baby, you didn't call me this morning. Is everything alright? Please call me back, I miss you." She then followed up with a text message.

Jazmine: Hey baby, what are you up to? Give me a call. I miss you.

She began doing laundry and reading about the psychological effects of taking anti-depressants and drinking alcohol. While Marcus's behavior had made her uncomfortable, she still wanted to help him to work out his issues. Two hours later her cell phone rang, and the Caller ID showed Marcus's name. She hesitated to answer but pushed the button right before it went to voice mail.

"Hello?"

"Hey Jazmine, I'm sorry I fell asleep on you last night. I must've been exhausted because I didn't even hear you leave."

Exhausted from doing what? You don't even have a job. It's more like you had too much to drink. "Do you even remember what happened before falling asleep?"

"Not much, I kind a remember you getting upset with me because you thought I was trying to hurt you. But I'd never do that. I don't remember much after that. Is everything okay? I know sometimes when I drink too much, I forget somethings that happened. If I disrespected you in anyway, I'm really sorry."

"It's no problem, I did feel uneasy though because you became a little aggressive, and you put your hands on me and shoved me backwards."

"I really need to get some help. I'd never mean to hurt you. Do you believe me?"

"I guess so, but I won't see you again until you get some help."

"I understand, Jazmine. I have a counselor I can call, so I'll set up an appointment for next week."

"Sounds good. I'm going to get back to my laundry, so I'll talk with you later."

"Okay, enjoy your day."

She considered taking a flight to Washington DC to surprise Noah the next weekend. It had now turned 3:00 and since Noah hadn't called her back, she sent another text message. "This is becoming a pattern," she said to herself. She called Erica to get her opinion but didn't get an answer. She got nervous and reached for her gun when she heard someone turn the key to enter her apartment. As she moved closer to the door, Noah came in with a bouquet of red roses. Right away she put the gun back in the drawer and stood there in disbelief.

"Oh my gosh! Noah, what are you doing here? I had no idea you were coming. I got so nervous, thinking, who the hell is that coming in here. I've been calling and texting you, but you didn't reply. How did you get here? I just can't believe this."

Noah stood there smiling, then picked her up and twirled her around.

"I know baby, I wanted to surprise you, that's why I didn't respond."

"You're so crazy." She smiled, as tears filled her eyes. "I love you so much."

"I love you too Jazz, please don't cry." He kissed her, then grabbed a tissue to wipe her tears. "Come on, let's sit down. Wow, baby, the apartment looks so nice. You did a great job in decorating it."

"Thanks, I'm glad you like it. It was kind of a challenge trying to add touches that might suit you, but I tried to do my best. After all, I'm usually here alone, so I added more things that I like."

"I hear you baby, but that will all change though."

"I hope so, but I won't go down that road right now. I'm just so glad to see you. You have no idea. Let me pull myself together. Are you hungry?"

"Yes, I can eat something."

She opened her refrigerator. "I have bagels, eggs, and some fruit, or I can make you a smoothie. You know me, I usually don't eat too much for breakfast."

"I'll have all of the above."

"Alright than, let me make my husband something to eat," she said, smiling.

During breakfast, they talked about everything from how well she'd decorated the apartment, to how much he wanted to finish the project and come home. He apologized over and over for not being there when she needed him. He reached for her every time she passed him, because he couldn't keep his hands off her. Jazmine was overjoyed in having him home and wanted to savor every moment, but Noah had other things on his mind. Instead, she just wanted to enjoy his company and cherish their time together.

Later that evening, they had a romantic dinner and drank wine under the moon light while viewing the bay bridge. His affection toward her had increased as he moved his chair closer to hers and began to make loving gestures.

"Noah, let's finish dinner first."

"Okay, okay," he said, smiling.

After dinner, they stood on the balcony to take in the view and enjoy the fresh air. He held her close to him as she melted into his arms, then led her into their bedroom. The ambiance had been set as candles were already lit throughout the apartment.

"Baby, I've missed you so much," he whispered.

"I've missed you too and I love you."

On one hand, she wanted to scold him for not being there for her, but she'd become too weak to resist him. She moaned for him to continue loving her while he took pleasure in satisfying her needs.

The next morning, they had breakfast on the balcony and laughed about the noise they'd made, and hoped it wasn't loud enough to disturb the neighbors.

"This view of the Bay Bridge is so awesome. I love the weather in Cali, and I couldn't have asked for a better apartment to live in. This makes me realize we could be enjoying a ride to San Francisco right now if I were home with you."

She tried blinking to keep her tears from falling when he reached for her. She didn't want to accept he'd be flying back to DC that morning.

"This will all be over soon, I promise Jazz."

"If you say so."

"Let's take some pictures before I leave," he said, pulling her closer to him. He blew in her ear to make her laugh, then snapped a couple of pictures while making funny faces. She always loved his sense of humor.

Silence filled the air on the way to the Oakland Airport. Although she'd wanted to express her concerns about him coming home, she chose to wait until later. When they arrived at the drop off point, they held each other tight, and kissed before saying goodbye.

"Call me when your plane lands in DC to let me know that you made it."

"Okay baby, I will. I love you."

"I love you too."

Jazmine rushed back home to get dressed to try and make it in time for church service. On the way there, she made a quick stop at Starbucks to grab a latte, when she'd came across Marcus getting out of his car.

"Hey there Jazmine, what a nice surprise. It looks like you're headed somewhere special. Do you have time to sit and have coffee with me?"

"Hey Marcus. No, not this time, I'm headed to church and I'm running a little late."

"I understand, I could use some church too." They laughed, then said their goodbyes after she paid for her coffee.

CHAPTER 7

Hanging in There

The preached message inspired Jazmine and helped to increase her faith. She'd started to lose hope, but it gave her the encouragement she needed to remain hopeful. After service, when Erica and her fiancé, Kevin, entered the lobby, she waved to get her attention.

"Hey Sis, how's it going?" Erica said.

"I'm doing better now. Noah gave me a surprise visit yesterday, which I really needed. I was beginning to lose faith in him. But I think things are going to be alright now."

"I'm so happy y'all got a chance to spend some time together. It's important to work hard at staying strong for each other. We need to get together for dinner or lunch soon."

Kevin had stopped to greet other church members when Erica waved for him to come over to where they were.

"Is it okay to tell Jazmine the good news?"

"Yes, of course," Kevin said.

"We've set our wedding date for this year, on October 16th, and we want you to be in our wedding."

"Oh, my goodness. Yes, I'd love too. Congratulations."

"Thank you so much. We have a lot to do, and I'll keep you updated as I start to make plans for our wedding. I'm so sorry Jazz, I'd love to stay and talk with you a little longer, but we have to run because we're meeting our family for lunch."

"I understand, I'll talk with you soon."

When they left, Jazmine began to reminisce about the kind of life she'd wanted with Noah. She rushed home and waited for his call, while going over her student's assignments. At 5:00, he still hadn't called. *His flight was scheduled to arrive at 3:00.* She got worried, but hesitated to call, instead she waited. At 7:30 her phone rang.

"Hey Noah, what's going on? I've been waiting for your call."

"Baby I'm sorry. I stopped by the office when I left the airport to complete some paperwork, and before I knew it, time had passed."

"Really. You know what Noah, I'm so damn tired of your excuses. I don't know who you think I am, but you better learn. When you tell me you're going to do something, you better do it or have a damn good reason why you didn't. You act like your job is more important than our marriage. I'm trying to give you space, so you can complete that project and bring your ass home, but this is getting too damn hard. I'll talk with you later." She hung up the phone before he could say another word. He called right back, but she didn't pick up.

The following two weeks, Jazmine focused on preparing assignments and joined a yoga class to help reduce her stress. She ignored text messages from Marcus, and despite Noah's apologies, she'd been short with him. She took Erica up on her suggestion to get together and wanted to include Sophia. She wanted to create some fun in her life and hanging out with her home girls would give her the kind of excitement she'd needed, so she followed up with her.

"Hey Erica, how're things going?"

"Hey Jazz, everything's going good. How're you?"

"I'm hanging in there. I was wondering if me, you, and Sophia can get together for lunch or dinner. It's been a long time since we've all hung out together."

"That sounds like fun. I've been thinking about that too," Erica said.

"Okay, hold on, I'll try to bring Sophia on the line so we can decide where and when to meet."

"Hello?"

"Hey Sophia, I have Erica on the other line. We're talking about getting together for lunch or dinner and we want you to join us."

"Yes, I'd love to. My life has been crazy, and I really need to get out and have some fun. Hey, remember when we use to go pole dancing?"

Jazmine and Erica laughed and said, "yes," in unison.

"What do y'all think about doing that again?" Sophia asked.

"Uh, we were a little younger then, and I've picked up a few pounds since then," Erica said.

Sophia chuckled. "Well, I've gained more weight than the two of you, so if I can do it then you can too."

"I can just see myself falling on my butt, but why not," Erica said.

They agreed to meet at the Phoenix Pole Dancing studio in Berkeley at 5:00 on Saturday. They arrived around the same time and greeted each other with hugs before going inside to register. After changing into their pole dancing gear, they stretched before getting on the poles.

"Who's going first?" Sophia asked. "Jazmine, you work out all the time, so why don't you go first."

"What, y'all can just jump on your own pole, and we can all do it together. Don't be scared?" Jazmine said, laughing.

"You're right let's do this. I'm not wasting my money," Erica said.

Five minutes later, they heard a loud thump. Jazmine and Erica jumped off their poles and ran over to check on Sophia. She laid on the floor laughing while trying to explain how her legs wouldn't stay around the pole like they used to.

"Okay, I'm not trying that again," Sophia said. "That's it for me."

"Are you okay?" they asked, while holding their lips closed, trying not to laugh.

"Yes, I'm fine. But I'm way too big to be doing this and I'm not as flexible as I used to be. So go ahead and finish your dancing, while I take a little break. Maybe I'll try it again in a few minutes or maybe not."

CHAPTER 8

Revealing Her Passion

After their pole dancing endeavor, Jazmine, Erica, and Sophia met at the Cheesecake Factory in Walnut Creek. The hostess greeted them and walked them to their table.

"Here you go," she said, handing them menus. "Your waiter will be with you shortly."

"Thank you," they replied.

"Well, I enjoyed trying to pole dance, but I definitely won't be doing that again," Erica said, while they busted out laughing.

"Now that's real talk, I did better than I thought I would, until I hit the floor," Sophia said, shaking her head. "We'll have to think of something else to do next time, like hiking. Now, we know for sure we're passed that stage. Although, Jazmine, I saw you were working that pole."

"Yeah, I did pretty good. I remembered how to grip the pole, plus I was determined. I've been so stressed out lately because of Noah being away, I'm doing all I can to fill that void. Y'all know how I studied psychology right? And how I have a passion for helping people deal with their problems. Well, lately I've been thinking about using my psychology skills to help someone."

Sophia and Erica listened while Jazmine tried to explain her desire to use her psychology skills.

"I'm sure it's difficult to deal with Noah being gone," Erica said.

"So, are you currently working with someone or how're you pursuing that? And being a teacher, do you really have time for that?" Sophia asked.

Jazmine became annoyed with Sophia's questions. She recalled past issues with her being too judgmental and blowing things out of proportion. Even though Sophia's curious personality had irritated her, she responded because she knew Sophia would have her back if necessary.

"Well, helping others have always been a passion of mine, so why not use the skills I've learned? This can also help to fill the void of Noah not being here. Yeah, yeah, I know I'm a teacher, but growing up I developed a sensitivity in helping others to work out their problems. So teaching is just an extension of my passion."

The waiter, a slender young man who appeared in his early twenties, sat three glasses of water on the table, then took their orders for appetizers. Jazmine's lack of response to Sophia's question about her latest endeavor created an awkward atmosphere, which only heightened her curiosity. Sophia posed the question to her again, but in a different way.

"So, Jazmine, can you share your latest project with us? I'm always curious how people get themselves in certain situations."

Yes, this is a project I'm pursuing. "Sure. Well, I ran into one of our old high school classmates. I'm not sure if you'll remember him. Do you remember Marcus? He was on the basketball team."

"Oh yes, I remember him. He was cute, but quiet and he seemed a little strange. Just not as talkative as his other teammates. Wasn't he voted most likely to succeed? It was interesting because when he was in my history class, he'd give an excellent debate, but besides that, he didn't talk much. So, what about him?" Sophia asked.

"Well, I ran into him at Starbucks a couple of weeks ago and since we realized...or so I thought, we work so close to each other, he asked if we could meet for lunch one day. So, we did, and everything went fine. But since then, he shared with me he'd lost his job and is having problems finding another one. Also, he's turned to prescription drugs and alcohol. So, I'm thinking maybe I can guide him in the right direction to get him the help he needs to get back on his feet," Jazmine explained.

"That's too bad. But you know, you must be careful in dealing with people with those kinds of issues. And if he decides to get belligerent, give us a call. I haven't given a good ass-whooping in a long time, and you know I'd enjoy doing that," Sophia said, chuckling.

"Yeah, Erica and I will put some karate chops on his behind if we need too. But I think he'll be fine. I'm not worried. I can take him myself if I have too. I didn't earn a black belt for nothing," Jazmine said, reflecting back to her high school days.

"For real, we may be older, but I'll never forget how to get somebody off of me, or y'all for that matter," Erica said, while scrolling through her phone.

Erica probably thinks I'm not being completely honest, but I'm not going to let her bother me. We all have our own way of dealing with things in life, Jazmine thought.

The waiter returned with their drinks, salads, and a basket of rolls, then took their prawn and french-fry orders. They made a toast to their continued friendship and took a quick sip of their drinks, except Jazmine took three sips.

"I really needed this drink," Jazmine said.

"Yes, there are times when a glass of wine is just what the doctor ordered," Erica said, smiling.

A few minutes later, Jazmine's mother-in-law called, whom she didn't care for, therefore she let it go to voice mail. His mom's controlling attitude towards Noah droved her crazy.

"Oh gosh, that was Noah's mom calling me. She probably tried to call him, and he didn't answer, so sometimes she'll call me to find out if I know where he is. I feel like saying he's in DC," she said, laughing. "I'll call her back later. I know she doesn't care for me, but I couldn't care less. She probably thinks I took her only son away from her. I don't know whose more self-centered, her or her son. And then there's his younger sister who she adores. I mean she's cute and all, but she's developed an attitude towards me. Since she turned thirteen, she just seems to be a little harder to get along with. Sometimes I feel like I married into straight chaos when it comes to his family."

"I hear you. I have my own issues that I'm dealing with so I can relate," Sophia said. We're supposed to be social distancing at church, but this chick keeps hanging onto David like she wants to be with him or something, so I'm going to have to address that issue without being put out the church."

"Oh really," Jazmine said.

"What's up with that?" Erica asked.

"Yes, every Sunday when we sing, she makes her way down from the choir stand to personally greet him with a hug. She completely ignores the fact that we're supposed to stay in our immediate area, and we're not supposed to be hugging each other even though we're vaccinated. She gon' make me come out of retirement. Y'all know I'm from the hood and I know how to take care of business. I guess she thinks because she's a little younger than me and still has her girlish figure, I'm going to be intimidated by her. We all know the saying, 'You can take the person out the hood, but you can't take the hood out the person.' I'll drag her ass all over that parking lot," Sophia said, while they busted out laughing.

By now they were all on their second round of drinks.

"Whew, she really don't want to mess with you, Jazmine said. Cuz out of all of us, you'll beat her ass first and ask questions later." They all started cracking up.

"Here you go. Three shrimp specials," the waiter said, sitting their plates on the table. "Can I get you anything else?"

"No thank you, I'm good," Erica answered.

"Everything's fine, thank you" Jazmine said, while Sophia nodded in agreement.

They laughed and talked about old times and realized they still had a strong bond. When they'd finished their meals, they agreed to get together at least once a month.

CHAPTER 9

Trying to Stay Optimistic

When Jazmine got in her car, she returned her mother-in-law's call.

"Hello?"

"Hi Mom. I'm sorry I missed your call. I was in a meeting. How're you?"

"Hey Jazmine, I'm doing good. I've just been trying to reach Noah. I've left a couple of messages, but he hasn't returned my calls. Have you spoken with him today?"

Jazmine recognized how she got right to the point and didn't bother to pay her the same respect in asking about her well-being.

"Um, I haven't spoken with him since last night. Is everything okay?"

"Yes. I just wondered when he was coming back home. I need him to help me with my yardwork. These weeds are growing like crazy in my backyard."

Jazmine shook her head, rolled her eyes, and wanted to drop the phone.

"Oh okay, I'll let him know when I talk with him."

"Please do. He used to always take good care of things around here for me, before he started working in DC."

You're not hurting for anything. Why don't you hire a gardener like everyone else does in your neighborhood? "Oh, I understand. How's Monique doing?"

"Monique is doing fine. We went shopping today and I bought her two new outfits, as if she needed more clothes. Would you like to speak with her?"

"Sure." Jazmine frowned but tried to sound enthusiastic.

"Hello?"

"Hey there Monique, how're you? It's been a while since we've talked."

"I'm good. Just missing my brother."

"Yeah, I hear you, me too. So, you went shopping today? Did you get some nice things?"

"Yep, sure did."

"Good for you. Okay, I just wanted to say hi and chat with you for a minute. Maybe we can get together and have lunch soon. How does that sound?"

"Uh, maybe, but I've been pretty busy lately. So, I don't know."

"I understand. We can talk about it later. You take care now. You can give the phone back to your mom unless she wants to talk later."

"Mom, she wants to know if you want to talk with her again."

"No. I'll just wait to hear back from Noah."

"She said she'll wait to hear back from my brother."

"That's fine. Take care Monique, and I hope to talk with you again soon."

"Okay bye." Monique hung up the phone without waiting for a response from her.

Jazmine did her best not to play into they're uppity attitude. She didn't appreciate how they treated her, but she had other ways of dealing with them. *They're so full of themselves. But it's cool, he's all mine and it ain't nothing they can do about it.*

"I'll be damned if I let Noah know she called," she said to herself. "They can kiss my ass."

Tears rolled down her face as she reminisced about her hopes of living a happy life with Noah.

She pulled out her phone to call him, then changed her mind and threw it on the passenger seat. When she began backing her Audi out of her parking stall, she'd just missed hitting a brand-new white BMW driving behind her. Startled by the horn from the other driver, she hit the brakes right away and drove back into her stall.

"Damn it. That was close," she said, shaking her head. *I'm such a nervous wreck.*

She sat there for a while and reflected on her wedding day and how she'd wanted to marry Noah despite his nonchalant attitude. She regretted how she'd ignored signs of him being too comfortable living in DC, even though she'd been warned by others of being too trusting. She always strived to do the right thing and didn't understand why Noah or anyone else would want to take advantage of that. Overcome with confusion and frustration, she began to believe maybe she'd been blowing her issues with Noah out of proportion. More than anything, she just wanted him to jump on a plane and come home. She tried to convince herself because he'd gain a significant commission check from the project, it would help in purchasing their new home. She resented him for not keeping his word in making sure to spend more time together. Perhaps using her psychology skills to help others would make her happy. She considered trying to spend time with her mother-in-law and his spoiled sister to help ease her anxiety, but she couldn't bring herself to try it.

It had become routine for her to take the long way home, as she did almost anything to fill her time. During her down time from handling schoolwork, she read suspense novels and watched movies on different streaming channels. Although she'd tried to adjust to being alone, it had become more challenging. Early that evening when her phone rang, she questioned who it might be, until she saw the caller ID.

"Hey Noah, you're calling early."

"Hey Jazze, how's my baby doing?"

"I'm good, surprised you're calling at this time. What are you up to?"

"Oh, do I have to be on a schedule to call only at a certain time?"

"No, of course not, it's just a little unusual."

"Well, I'm going to hang out with some of my coworker's tonight, so I thought I'd give you a call a little earlier."

"I see. So, you're getting into the partying game?"

"No, it's not like that. It's one of the guy's birthdays, so we're going to a casino to play a few games and maybe shoot some pool."

"Oh, so you're going to do some gambling?"

"Just a little."

"I see." Jazmine reflected on when he used to have a problem with gambling.

When they dated, she learned that Noah had developed a passion for gambling but convinced him to cut back. Because he now lived in DC, she had no control over how often he went to the casino. He also used to gamble on-line, and on occasion he'd fly to Las Vegas. Her concern began to increase, and she needed to find a way to keep his gambling under control.

CHAPTER 10

Making Up for Lost Time

A week later, Jazmine flew to DC to give Noah a surprise visit. She'd become even more uneasy with the stability of their marriage, therefore she wanted to spice things up a bit. She also needed to convince herself that his gambling hadn't become an issue again. She arrived on Saturday morning hoping to catch him still at home. After the plane landed at the Washington National Airport, she went to the pick-up area for Uber drivers. Once she'd confirmed the sticker on the car and the uber driver's identification, a well-groomed older gentleman, with a southern accent got out to greet her and helped with her luggage.

"Hello, my name is Samuel."

"Hi, I'm Jazmine."

"Let me help you with your luggage."

"Thank you. I just have the one piece."

When she got in the car, she called Noah, but it went to voice mail. Instead of leaving a message, she hung up. *I'm just going to surprise him like he did me.* She hoped he'd be happy to see her. Fifteen minutes later they arrived at his apartment building.

"Okay, we're here," the Uber driver said.

"Thank you."

"Sure, let me get your luggage for you."

Jazmine got out of the car and passed him a tip.

"Here you go and thanks again."

"Thank you. Enjoy your trip."

"I will, have a nice day."

She tried to call Noah again, but he didn't pick up. *Goodness, I hope I didn't make a mistake in showing up without letting him know. Maybe he's in the shower.*

The apartment security guard, a soft-spoken young lady with bright red hair, greeted her when she entered the building.

"Hello, how're you?"

"Hello, I'm good, how're you?" Jazmine replied, pushing the button to get on the elevator.

When the elevator stopped for her floor, she became nervous while walking closer to his apartment. She sat her luggage on the floor and opened her purse to search for her keys. "Damn it.

I left the key on the table." She sighed. *Oh well, so much for the surprise act I'd planned.*

After ringing and knocking on the door several times with no answer, she called his phone again, but the voice mail came on. "Hey Noah, it's me. I'm at your apartment. I was trying to surprise you. If you're inside, please open the door." *Goodness where can he be?*

She sat on her luggage and waited for an hour, then headed downstairs to find a more comfortable seat. The security guard shift had changed to a handsome middle-aged gentleman with dark brown curly hair, who had a big smile.

"Good morning. I'm here to visit my husband but he's not answering the door. So, is it okay if I sit here in the lobby for a while?"

"Sure, that's fine."

"Thank you. I won't be doing a surprise visit again." She sighed, while sitting on the black leather sofa.

"Yeah, that can be risky. Would you like a magazine and some water?"

"Yes, thank you."

He got up and handed her the items.

"Thank you, I appreciate it."

"You're welcome. Do you mind if I ask, is it a special occasion, the reason you're surprising him?"

"No, I just thought it'd be nice."

"Oh, I see."

Ten minutes later, Noah walked through the glass door with his shirt hanging out of his pants and his tie loose.

"Oh, my goodness, Jazmine. What, what are you doing here? I mean, is everything okay?"

"Yes, everything's fine Noah. I just wanted to surprise you that's all."

"Baby that's so nice of you. I was just going to give you a call when I got in." He bent down to give her a hug, but she moved away. "Let me get your luggage."

"Thank you again for the water, and have a good day," she said to the security guard.

"No problem, you have a good day as well."

Noah turned back and glanced at the guard before getting on the elevator.

"Why didn't you let yourself in?"

"Because I accidently left the key at home. You know how I hate having too many keys on my keychain. But this is a real lesson, and I won't be doing this again. So, it looks like you've been out all night."

"Well, I went to a casino with some friends last night, and time got away from me."

"So, you were up all night, gambling?"

"Come on, Jazmine, don't get on my case. What do you expect me to do, sit in this apartment all the time? I'm going to take a quick shower. I'll be right back."

"Yeah alright."

After his shower, he sat on the couch next to her and put his arm around her. His body still warm and damp from the shower and the fresh scent of his cologne invaded her senses. Out of frustration, she wanted to push him away when he began kissing her, but she didn't have the strength.

"Jazz, I've missed you so much. I'm sorry I wasn't home when you got here, but I'll make it up to you."

She craved his affection, and no amount of frustration would change her desire to fulfill her needs, at least, not this time. Noah took his time and continued kissing her when his navy-blue terry cloth towel dropped to the floor. To remind him of what he'd been missing, she'd come prepared in how to seduce him, by wearing the two-piece Victoria Secret set he loved. After they made love, two hours later, they'd fallen asleep holding each other. Later that evening, they ordered pizza, then continued their romance into the night. The next morning, he woke up to the aroma of bacon and pancakes.

"Hey there sleepy head. Are you hungry? I made us breakfast," she said.

"Hey beautiful, thank you. Yes, I could use some food. My energy is kind a low right now," he said, holding her from behind with his arms around her waist.

"Well, we did make up for lost time, didn't we?"

Despite being irritated in having to wait for him to come home and his non-response to her phone calls, she'd made it a point to remain calm the rest of the day.

CHAPTER 11

A Promotion Offer

The next day, Jazmine woke-up early with questions on her mind that she needed answers to before heading back to California. Although hesitant to discuss her concerns because of the great time they were having, her determination fueled her. She worried about how to start a conversation with him about gambling and the impact it might have on their relationship. *I'll definitely get some answers to my questions before I leave.* While she prepared omelets and roasted potatoes for breakfast, Noah came into the kitchen.

"Hey there, I didn't hear you get up. You were sleeping like a baby. But I figured the smell of breakfast would get you moving. My plane leaves at 1:30, so I wanted to get an early start," she said.

"Awe man, I thought you were leaving tonight. Maybe you can change it to a later flight."

"Hm, I can always call the airline to find out."

"Please do. I'm just not ready to say good-bye yet."

"I'll call right after we finish breakfast. It's only 9:30, so it should be plenty of time for them to change my flight. So, let's eat."

"Yes ma'am. It looks good baby."

"So, how much did you make the other night?"

"Huh?"

"How much money did you make?"

"I made a little, not as much as I wanted to make. But there's always a next time."

"What's a little?"

"Wow. You sure do have a lot of questions, like, a couple of hundred."

"So how much did you lose?"

"I basically broke even."

"Sure, you did. I'd been trying to reach you, and I was afraid something happened to you. I kept calling and calling and you didn't answer your phone. I guess you were having too much fun."

"I probably still have it on silent and didn't hear it ringing. Let me check," he said, pulling his phone out of his jacket. "Uh, sorry about that. But I definitely was planning on calling you when I got in. I must say this is a nice surprise though."

"So, you were up all-night gambling?" she said, lifting a forkful of potatoes.

"Again, I'm not going to sit in this apartment alone every night, Jazz."

"You seem different Noah, I don't know what's going on. And your attitude is so nonchalant and uncaring."

"Come on Jazmine, let's not get all deep with things. I just go out sometimes to have fun. What's the big deal?"

"I'm just not understanding you, Noah. You used to have a problem with gambling, now it sounds like you're falling back into that trap. I'm not going to let your selfishness get in the way of our marriage. This whole living apart thing have been hard enough for me, now you're bringing this into the picture. It's just too much."

"So, you think I'm being selfish. Wow, you know you can always move here with me. That way we can be together."

"What the hell are you talking about? We agreed you'd move back to California after this project was completed. You know how I feel about living far away from my parents. So, it sounds like you're not coming back home any time soon?"

"Well, I was going to tell you today, I was offered a promotion within my department and I'm thinking about accepting it."

Tears filled her eyes while she tried to remain calm. "Wait. What. Are you kidding? A promotion? But you can't accept a promotion."

"Don't cry Jazz. Listen, the job will allow me to work from home at times and it pays really well."

"What does 'at times' mean?" She picked up her napkin to catch her tears before they fell.

"I'm not quite sure yet, but I'll find out. Look at it this way. We can build our savings even faster now that you're working and with my potential promotion."

"I don't know Noah. I wasn't expecting this. We've been going through this for too long and I'm really getting tired of it. This is all so ironic. I came down to surprise you, but in turn, I got surprised."

"Come on Jazz, believe me, it'll all work out. Now, let's enjoy this nice breakfast you made. So, how're things working out at the school?"

"Don't try to change the subject, Noah. I've been patient in waiting for you to come home. Now I have to deal with worrying about you gambling all our money away, and a possible promotion." She sighed. "If it's not one thing with you, it's another."

"Look, I'll find out more about this promotion, and we can talk more about it later."

"Yeah, sure Noah. My job at the school is going fine. I'm adjusting to the summer school program and surprisingly, most of the students are eager to learn."

"Well, I'm not at all surprised. I knew you'd make a great teacher and I'm sure the students enjoy having you there."

Because Jazmine's frustration had gotten the best of her, she exaggerated while trying to explain her other interests.

"By the way, I've started using my psychology skills to help out one of my old classmates from high school."

"Oh wow, that's great Jazz. You've always been sensitive to the needs of others, which is one of the things that attracted me to you, besides your beauty of course. You're very good at listening, which is all most people need."

"I try. I really didn't think you noticed that about me."

"Baby, I notice everything about you. So, what are they dealing with?"

"They lost their job and have now turned to drinking and taking prescription drugs."

"Hm, sounds like they need to be in an AA program."

"Yes, they do, and I think they realize that, so I'm just trying to coach them along."

"I see, is this a male or female?"

"Um, it's a female. Her name is Marsha. I met her at—"

"Marsha? You've never been good at lying Jazmine."

"Okay, okay, his name is Marcus. He was a classmate in high school. He never hung out much but played on the basketball team. I saw him at Starbucks one day and we chatted for a while. When I asked how things were going since high school, he explained things had changed for the worst after being laid off from a major corporation. He said it hasn't been easy finding another job and was having a hard time dealing with it. So, I thought maybe I'd help him in working through his issues."

"But Jazz, you don't have any experience in working with people with alcohol problems. Are you spending time with him?"

"Not really, I just emailed him some information about the effects of mixing alcohol and drugs, and I gave him some material on grounding exercises. Hopefully, he'll apply those practices which can help him to get his life back on track."

Jazmine made it a point to be vague about her relationship with Marcus.

"Well, be careful, Jazz. I don't want you to think you can help everyone and end up in a bad situation. And being that I'm not there to help you, it bothers me you can be harmed in dealing with someone you really don't know."

"Yes, I understand what you're saying, but so far I haven't had any problems."

"Like I said, be careful. You really don't know him."

"Okay Noah. Let's get back to you. What casino are you spending your time at these days?"

"I go to the MGM most times, but baby please, we only have a few more hours together, so let's not argue."

"I just want you to understand how I feel, Noah. Nothing seems to be sinking in."

"Trust me, I understand. And I'll let you know more about the promotion when I find out more information."

Jazmine granted his wishes because she didn't want to leave on a bad note. Taking a later flight gave them much needed time to relax and rekindle their love for each other. She had a smooth noneventful flight and called Noah when she got home.

"Hey baby, I made it home."

"Good. How was your flight?"

"Thank goodness, it was actually a pretty smooth ride. I'm getting more use to it, since it seems that's the only way, I'm going to see you."

"Stop, it'll all work out, I promise. I'm glad you came to visit me. I can't wait to hold you in my arms again. Jazmine, you know I love you, right?"

While talking to Noah, a text message came through from Marcus updating her on his progress, but she didn't reply. She hit the speaker button and sat down with her head in her hands.

"Yes, I know, but this is driving me crazy. Coming home to an empty apartment and all, it... it just doesn't feel right, Noah."

"I know it doesn't, and I'm sorry, but I'll be home for good soon."

"Yeah, okay, I'm going to get settled and I'll call you back later. Love you."

"Okay, I love you too."

CHAPTER 12

Trying to Help

Jazmine had fallen asleep early after eating a small salad and drinking a glass of wine. Exhausted from the drama she'd gone through in DC; she'd forgotten to call Noah back. At 1:00 am she reached for her phone to call him, then changed her mind. At 8:00 am, she'd received two text messages from Marcus but didn't reply. *I can't deal with this right now. What the hell is wrong with this guy? Maybe I should just leave that fool alone and let him get help from someone else.*

The next two weeks were challenging for her. Noah had accepted the promotion despite her concerns. Although it had a substantial increase in pay, but at what cost? He needed to get accustomed to his new position and being a director required a lot more attention than she'd expected. Saturday morning, she received a call from Marcus.

"Hello?"

"Hey Jazmine, how're things going? I've been trying to contact you and hoped we could meet for lunch or dinner. I got a little concerned when you didn't reply to my text messages. Is everything okay?"

"Yes, I've just been busy with my students, so things have been a little hectic with assignments. How're things going with you?"

"I've been good, trying to find a job and I've rejoined the twelve-step program to help me get back on track. It's been a challenge, but I know it's what I must do to get my life in order. I was hoping we could get together for dinner this evening?"

"Sure. Why not."

"Okay, good. I was thinking of having Italian food. How does that sound?"

"Sounds good. I haven't had pasta in a while."

"How about meeting at Gypsy's Trattoria Italiana, on Durant, at 6:00? Their food is pretty good."

"Oh yes, I like their food. I'll be there."

She began to question her relationship with Marcus. "What am I doing?" she asked herself. *The last time I saw him he acted a little nutty. Well, at least we're eating out and not at his place. Maybe this can be an opportunity to start using my psychology skills to help him get back on track.*

Prior to meeting for dinner, she pulled out reading material on the effects of mixing prescription drugs and alcohol. She read chapter after chapter and came across grounding exercises to share with him. After she'd finished reading, she took a nap, and woke up to a chime ringtone on her phone. A text message had come through from Marcus at 5:45.

"Darn it, what time is it?" she said to herself.

She jumped up and got dressed, then replied to his text letting him know she'd be running a little late. When she arrived, he'd been sitting at the table drinking a cup of coffee. He stood up and greeted her with a warm hug, then pulled her chair out. A slightly plump waitress, wearing bright red lipstick approached their table.

"Would you like something to drink?" she asked.

"I'll have a Pepsi please," Jazmine said.

"Sir, would you like something else besides coffee?"

"Yes, I'll have a Pepsi as well."

"Okay, I'll be right back with your drinks and some bread, unless you're ready to place your order for dinner?"

"As a matter of fact, I am. I'll have the chicken marsala please," Jazmine said.

"And for you sir?"

"I'll have the spaghetti with meat balls."

"I'll put those orders in for you and I'll be back shortly."

"Thank you," they said, in unison.

"I'm sorry for running late, I've been a little exhausted lately."

"No problem, I understand."

Right away, she'd wanted to ask about the twelve-step program and his job hunting but decided to wait until later in the conversation.

"So, how've you been?" he asked. "It's been a little while since we've gotten together."

"I've been good, just working hard. I love teaching, but it can be a challenge in getting some students motivated to do their best."

"I'm sure it can be hard when you're doing all you can to keep them on the right track. But you can only do so much, it's ultimately up to the student."

"You're right about that."

The waitress sat their drinks with a basket of warm bread and butter on the table, and shortly after returned with their meals.

"I'd like to give thanks for our food," Jazmine said.

"Yes of course."

They had light conversation while eating dinner. Later, she asked, "so, are things going good with your program?"

"Yes, it's going well. It's been only a couple of weeks, but I plan to stick with it this time, so that I can be stronger than I was when I left before."

"Yes, that's a good idea. It'll give you a fresh start in your life." She wanted to show her support but not go overboard.

"I was wondering if I can count on you to help me stay on track. Right now, I'm feeling strong, but I just don't know how long that's going to last. I don't want to have a relapse like before, so I can use all the help I can get."

"I see."

"Uh oh, that doesn't sound to promising."

"Well, I hear where you're coming from, and I do know some things about helping you to get back on track. But ultimately, it's up to you. You have to want to get yourself together. I don't mean to sound insensitive. I'm just saying you have to be committed because no matter what I do, *you* have to want to change."

"Yes, I know, and I'm going to do whatever I need to do to get through this."

"So, it sounds like you're comfortable with how the program is coming along so far?"

He squinted his eyes and took a deep breath.

She raised her eyebrows. "Oh, I'm sorry. I thought since you asked for my support, you'd be willing to talk about how things were going."

"Again, it's only been a couple of weeks. But it's going well. Like I said, it's going to get more challenging as time goes on, so I hope I can count on you for support."

"But like I said, I can only do so much. As a matter of fact, I brought you some information about grounding exercises to help you along with the program. This shows eight different physical techniques you can do when you're feeling overwhelmed. Just to give you an idea, they involve deep breathing, stretching, exercising, mindfulness, and senses. I'd like you to read this information because it can be beneficial in helping you to stay focused."

"Wow, thank you so much Jazmine. That's so sweet of you to do this. They give us this type of information in the program, but I haven't applied it yet. This only reinforces the importance of sticking with it. Your husband is a lucky man."

"True, but why do you say that?"

"You're a sweet person for taking the time to try and help a person like me. Besides that, you're beautiful inside, and out. I really messed up on my marriage. You remind me a lot of my ex-wife; she was very kind-hearted in extending herself to helping others. You do have to be careful though, there are some loons out here. You can't be too naïve because you can end up in an unsafe situation."

"I'm really sorry your marriage didn't work out. But you never know, maybe you two will get back together later."

"Who knows, maybe so."

The waitress approached their table and asked, "would you like to look at the dessert menu?"

"No thank you. I'm good," Jazmine said.

"Are you sure you don't want coffee or dessert?" he asked.

"Nah, I've had enough. I need to head back home but thanks for asking."

"Sure, I understand, hopefully we can get together again soon."

"Thank you for the nice dinner," she said as they approached her car.

"Sure, I always enjoy spending time with you, " he said, holding her door as she got in. "Is it alright if I call you in a few days, just to keep you updated on my progress?"

"Yes, it's fine."

"Thank you again for having dinner with me. I realize the last time we were together things didn't turn out right. But I want to make things right going forward. Drive safe, Jazmine."

"It's okay. I sure will. Good-bye."

Marcus loved the response he'd gotten from her, because no one had shown him that much attention in a long time. He'd distance himself from all his family because of the embarrassment in losing his job. Her support gave him a sense of hope and belief that maybe he'd live a normal life again.

CHAPTER 13

Lord Help Me

Although Jazmine agreed to support Marcus, her real focus involved getting Noah back home. Erica had tried to convince her of the importance of Noah's job and the undivided attention it might require. She explained how it's going to take patience, but Jazmine had other plans. She'd struggled to remain understanding while he got adjusted to his new position, and she couldn't let go of the promise he'd made to her. His focus had changed, and she wanted answers to the shift in his attitude and lack of consideration. Their promise to work together, save for a new home and have children had no longer been a topic of discussion.

When she returned from taking her Saturday morning jog, she made a cup of coffee, and opened her laptop to check their bank account. At first, his bi-weekly deposits were three thousand dollars, but as of late they'd become less than normal. She didn't want to confront him, but she needed to get to the bottom of why he'd been inconsistent with his deposits. At 10:00 am, she checked her phone to make sure she hadn't missed his call. *Here we go, he always calls me like clockwork on Saturday mornings.* At noon she still hadn't heard from him, and out of instinct, she gave him a call.

"Hey baby, how's it going? I didn't hear from you this morning. I miss you. Give me a call back, love you."

She became worried as more hours passed. He hadn't mentioned anything about going into work when they talked the night before. *He'd better not be out gambling our savings away.* At 3:00 she tried calling him again, but it went to voicemail. Ten minutes later, her phone rang.

"Hey Noah."

"Hey Jazz, how's it going?"

"I've been worried, where have you been?"

"Uh, I overslept. And then I went out for a late jog and uh—"

"Hm, you sound tired."

"I do? Well, I am a little."

"Did you forget to make the deposit to our account?"

"Wait, I didn't make it? Oh wow, I completely forgot. I'll do it first thing Monday morning."

"Did you go out after we talked last night?"

"Yeah, for a little while."

"Where did you go?"

"I just went to the casino for a while."

"Hm, it's obvious you have a problem. You better not have spent your paycheck on playing that damn poker. How long has this been going on Noah?"

"What, I just do it for fun. You're blowing this out of proportion."

"I know one damn thing, that money better be in the account on Monday."

"And if it's not, then what?"

"Have you lost your damn mind, saying that to me? Then your ass is mine that's what. You know how I do. Don't play with me Noah."

"You must be drinking Jazmine. Don't you think it's a little early for that?"

"You have a lot of nerve, like I said, the money better be in the account on Monday."

She hung up the phone before he could say another word.

"That jerk. What…what the hell is wrong with him? I can't deal with this," she said, pacing the floor. "It's like he's a different person. He'd better get it together or it's over. He's just trying to deflect, asking me if I'm drinking. I'm sick of him and Marcus. Here I am trying to help a friend with issues, now I have to deal with my own husband's addiction problems."

Monday morning, she woke up with swollen eyes and too embarrassed to go into work. She considered staying home but didn't want to call out sick at the last minute. While the students took their tests, she spent most of the time preoccupied about her problems with Noah.

"Ms. Wright, can I talk with you for a minute please?" one of her students asked.

"Sure, Simone."

"Wait. Are you okay?" Simone asked, seeing that her eyes were swollen.

"Yes, Simone, I am. What can I help you with?"

"Um, I had a hard time studying this week because I found out my cousin has the corona virus. A couple of days ago he had a hard time breathing and is now in the hospital. I'm really hoping he doesn't have to be put on a ventilator. So, I've been very distracted. How much will this affect my final grade?"

"I'm sorry to hear that, Simone. I hope and pray he starts to get better soon. So, to keep your grade average up, you'll need to do good in passing this test. Just do your best and you'll be fine. I understand you're worried, but you're smart, and I know you'll do well, just try to concentrate and take your time."

"Thank you, Ms. Wright, I appreciate your confidence in me."

"You're welcome, Simone."

Jazmine often scanned the classroom to check for anyone struggling or had questions but were too shy to ask. She found one student gazing up with his hand on his chin.

"Isaiah, do you have any questions?"

"No thank you, Ms. Wright, I'm good. I was just thinking about how to work this problem. But I think I got it now."

"Good. Class, you have fifteen minutes left, so stay focused."

Although Jazmine struggled to concentrate, her determination to be there for her students is what motivated her. She'd considered taking a jog or a walk after class but didn't have the energy. She dreaded checking their bank account again because she'd feared Noah hadn't made the deposit. *I should have confronted him sooner about his past inconsistencies, instead I overlooked them. Not smart Jazmine.*

Overcome from embarrassment and disrespect, she'd planned to give him an ultimatum. While gathering papers on her desk, she thought, *either he comes home soon or it's over. He thinks he can put me on a damn shelf and take me off to play with me when he gets ready. If things don't work out the way he promised, I'm going to karate chop his behind like he was my worst enemy. Lord help me...*

"Alright class, time's up. Please bring your test papers forward, and you're dismissed. Thank you and enjoy the rest of your day."

CHAPTER 14

Feeling Embarrassed

Crying every other day had become the norm for Jazmine. Noah had humiliated her by turning her life upside down. She'd been filled with aspirations of living a happy life with him and raising children together, but that had become a distant likelihood. She never expected to be in that situation and needed to talk to someone. Sharing her concerns with her girlfriends made her uneasy because she didn't want him to be judged by them. But she needed to find a way to stop their relationship from falling apart.

When she got home from work, she sat on her cushiony sofa, rested her feet on the ottoman and put her head back. "Ah, it feels so good to be home," she said to herself. She checked their bank account and found he'd made the deposit, but made three withdrawals right after, bringing the deposit down to four-hundred dollars. Not only did he take money from his deposits, but he also took money from the deposits she'd made. *My gosh, what the hell is he doing? I can't do this.* She picked up her phone to call him, but the voice mail came on.

"Noah, call me back, I need to talk with you." She was beside herself and tried to figure out who to confide in. *I need to talk to someone. I can't tell my mom, so I'll call Erica.* With tears in her eyes, she dialed her number.

"Hello?"

"Hi sis, I need to talk with you."

"Jazz are you alright? What's wrong?"

"Yes and no. I'm so pissed at Noah right now. I want to hurt him. He keeps playing games with me and I'm so damn tired of it."

"Wait, calm down a minute. What happened?"

"Erica, he's spending all our savings on gambling, and I can't deal with this. I just checked our bank account, and... and all our savings are practically gone. I mean, I knew he liked to gamble but I just didn't see this coming."

"My goodness, I'm so sorry Jazz. What the hell is going on with him? Have you talked with him about it?"

"Yes, I've tried talking with him because things are starting to get out of hand. I hate arguing with him, and I guess I didn't want to believe he's started gambling again. I just thought he'd gotten passed that, but I should've known better. Now he just blows me off like I'm being a nag."

"Wow, this sounds serious. He needs to stop gambling and get some help if it's that big of a problem."

"You're right, he needs help, but I doubt if he'll get it or even admit that he needs it. I just left him a voice mail because we need to figure this out. Honestly, Erica, this is really getting old, and I don't think our marriage can survive this."

"I understand what you're saying Jazz. But try to hang in there. You know how I feel about the unity of marriage, but it does take two to make it work. I really feel bad for you. You're so strong and have been stretching your patience with him. I don't even know if I could deal with…sorry I didn't mean it like that. I'm just saying, he needs to get a grip and do what he needs to do to make it work. Even if it means seeing a counselor, then so be it."

"It's fine. It's a lot and I appreciate your support. I'm really trying to be strong, so I'll see how it goes. I'll keep you posted," she said, wiping away her tears.

"Don't hurt him, Jazz. I know how you can be."

"I'll try not to," she said, sighing.

"You promise?"

"That's asking a lot, Erica, but I'll try not to. I just can't guarantee anything at this point. This is all so embarrassing. So again, I don't know sis. It's even getting hard for me to concentrate at work."

"You'll be okay, just try to relax for now, and call me any time. Let's get together soon."

"Okay, I'll try."

"Well, what about dinner this Sunday after church, unless you want to get together sooner?"

"Okay, it'll have to just be me and you though, I can't deal with Sophia right now. I know she means well, but who knows how she'll respond to this situation, and I'm so on the edge right now. That wouldn't be good for either of us."

"I hear you. I won't mention it to her."

"Thanks. We can decide on where to go when I see you on Sunday. Right now, I need to lie down because I have a terrible headache."

"Okay, get some rest and I'll check on you later."

"I will. Thank you again Erica."

"No thanks needed. You're my sis and I'm here for you no matter what."

Convinced Noah had been playing her and taking her kindness for granted, Jazmine wanted to show him she could be just as mean as she was nice. And although she might've been naïve to some things, she wasn't naïve to all things. *My goodness, I'm just all over the place. One minute I'm angry with him, the next minute I want to make things right. I need to figure out how to get this under control, because it's obvious he's not listening to me.*

While soaking in the tub, she read about the effects of gambling issues which blew her away. *Could he really be in this deep? Wow, based on what I'm reading, my husband needs help, but how can I help him when he's so far away.* Sharing his gambling problem with his mom wasn't an option, plus she didn't want her to know how serious it had become.

"If I keep going down this road, I'm going to need some counseling myself," she said to herself.

Her stress level continued to increase while she searched on-line for information about problems with gambling. She read late into the night, trying to find out the best way to help him. When she woke up in the middle of the night, she'd reached for her phone to call him again, then changed her mind. She turned over her wet pillow and pulled the cover over her head. *What's going on, is this really happening?*

The next morning, she woke up exhausted, but forced herself to take a jog before heading into work. She'd no idea Marcus was inside Starbucks watching as she jogged. When she reached a certain distance, he grabbed his coffee and keys and rushed to his car to follow her. He kept his distance and once she reached her apartment, he'd parked his car in an obscure area. He tried to get a view of which apartment she entered when she ran up the stairs, but she'd stepped out of his view.

CHAPTER 15

A Loaded Question

*N*oah *still hasn't returned my call.* Jazmine wanted to call him, but instead she waited until he called her back. She jumped in the shower to get ready for work, then heard her phone rang while getting dressed. *Who could be calling me this early? Maybe Noah finally decided to return my call,* she thought, then noticed Marcus's name.

"Hello?"

"Hi Jazmine, how're you? It's so nice to hear your voice."

"Hey Marcus, you're calling me so early. What's up?"

"I just wanted to update you on my progress. My program is going well, and I was thinking maybe we could go out for a short while to celebrate. I'd like that a lot."

"Look, I don't know, Marcus. I have a lot going on right now, and I'm just not in the mood to go out."

"I see. Is everything alright?"

"That's a loaded question. You know what Marcus? I really want to see you get through your program successfully, but right now I just can't help you like I'd like to. So, with that being said, I'll call you when things are better on my end."

He took a deep breath. "I understand, but right now I don't have any support and I just thought you might be willing to stick this out with me. At least that's the impression I got when I last saw you."

"You don't have any family to help you? I don't mean to sound inconsiderate, but right now is just not a good time. Just give me a few days to get my thoughts together. I may reach out to you later in the week."

"If you insist. It doesn't sound like there is anything I can say to change your mind."

"Nope, not right now."

Jazmine's response appeared cold toward Marcus. He wanted to find a way to change her mind, instead he accepted there might be a chance for them to talk again later. After hanging up, she called Noah.

"Hey there, you didn't call me back last night. Did you work late or something?" She wanted to give him the benefit of the doubt, even though she believed he'd been out gambling.

"Yeah, I worked late and when I got home, I was tired and fell right to sleep."

"What do you mean you worked late? Noah, stop lying. You know you were out gambling again. So, how do you suppose we fix this? You have a problem, and we need to get a handle on it, or we won't be able to survive this."

"Well, I—"

"Well, I, nothing. You either decide to get help or we're just not going to make it."

"Okay, okay, I hear you. But I don't think it's as bad as you're saying."

"Really. Then why are you spending our savings? Are you on drugs or something?"

"Hell no. Jazmine, how can you say that?"

"Wow, so you're spending all of our savings on gambling. Do you even realize how much money you've spent? Our savings account is practically down to zero compared to how it was before. What about the house we planned to buy? Is that not important to you any more Noah? This is so frustrating. You're turning our lives upside down, and I don't know how to stop it. If you're not willing to stop what you're doing I, I just don't know what else to say."

"Jazmine, please calm down. We're going to be fine. I'll slow down and I'm sorry for dipping into our savings."

"Dipping is not the word. Now we have to start all over in saving our money. So, are you going to get some help or what?"

"I will, if you really think I should."

"Wait, you have to accept that you have a problem, or you'll never stop."

"I guess I do because I never meant to touch our savings. So where do I go from here?"

"I'll do some research in your area and try to locate a place where you can get some help. Noah, this is serious. You must follow through with this because the path you're on is not good. I really wish you were here, or I was there, so we can work this out together. I hate that you accepted that new promotion because you could be home by now. This separation is ruining our marriage."

He sighed and kept quiet.

"Do you hear me? Either you get some help, or everything we worked for will just go down the drain."

"Yes, I hear you, Jazmine, but I have to get to work. I'll call you back this evening."

"You promise?"

"Yes, I promise. I love you."

"I love you too."

Jazmine wanted to understand his situation of being alone and his desire to get out and have fun, but she didn't expect him to start gambling again. When they got married, she understood his love for gambling, but never imagined it'd become that serious. She doubted he'd get the help he needed and blamed him for letting it get out of hand. While researching different counseling programs in the DC area, she'd hoped to find a reputable program to help him, and not someone just out to make money. For the first time, she accepted he'd become addicted, and the affects were detrimental to their marriage and all he'd worked for. She spent three days calling and comparing rates with different counseling services. All of that had taken a toll on her, and she had no other choice, but to try and help him. In her research she learned there were seven different types of gambling disorders. There's the Professional Gambler—Casual Gambler—Serious Social Gambler— Relief and Escape Gambler— Conservative Gambler—Personality Gambler and a Compulsive Gambler. Jazmine became overwhelmed with frustration as she tried to come to grips with his addiction. *My gosh, this is a lot, and I have no idea which one he is, but I'm going to hang in there and try to help him.*

CHAPTER 16

Feeling Vulnerable

Two weeks later, Noah agreed to meet with a well-known counselor in the downtown DC area. Jazmine was at her wits end in trying to convince him he needed counseling. She tried to compartmentalize her life to keep her sanity, but her frustration only got worse. She wanted revenge for the embarrassment he'd put her through but continued to suppress that desire. In the meantime, Marcus had completed his twelve-step program and wanted to celebrate and share the good news with her. Hearing good news could be the distraction she needed while dealing with her issues with Noah. She concluded if he didn't get it together, she'd start living the single life that she'd become use to. Friday morning, on her way to work she received a text message from Marcus.

Marcus: Hey Jazmine, I hope you're doing well. I know you told me to wait until I heard back from you before we talked again. But I just thought you'd be willing to help me celebrate the completion of my program. Is it possible to get together for dinner tomorrow night?

Jazmine: Yes, it is. I'm really happy you completed your program.

Marcus: Great, I can make reservations at Scott's Seafood Grill & Bar in Jack London Square for 7:00. Is that okay?

Jazmine: Yes, that's fine. I'll be there.

Marcus: Thank you, Jazmine. I really appreciate it.

Jazmine: It's okay, I know this means a lot to you.

Marcus made it a point to ask for a seat in a secluded area where there were minimal distractions. Their evening together went better than she'd expected. He appeared healthier and confident in how his life had changed for the better. She believed he wanted to have a closer relationship because he'd said all the right things. Her spirits were lifted when he gifted her with a card and a bouquet of yellow roses for supporting him. She wanted to order a glass of wine, but out of concern that it might cause him to relapse, she decided against it. The ambiance and the background music were mellow enough to help her relax.

"Thank you so much for the beautiful roses and the nice card."

"You're welcome. I'm glad you accepted my offer to celebrate with me."

"Sure, you deserve it. I'm happy to share this time with you. That is a great accomplishment."

A cheerful waitress approached their table with water, warm bread, and a dipping sauce.

"Good evening, would you like an appetizer and something else to drink?" she asked.

"No thank you, but I am ready to place my order. I'll have the petite filet mignon with a coke please," Jazmine said.

"And for you sir?"

"I'll have the same, with a coke as well."

"Okay, I'll put that order in for you and I'll be back shortly."

"Thank you," Marcus said.

"I really want to thank you for believing in me. You don't realize how much your support helped me to believe in myself. We met at a troubled time in my life, and you didn't shy away like a lot of people have done. Jazmine, you don't realize it, but I feel at peace when I'm around you."

"Okay Marcus, slow down. I mean, I haven't done anything."

"But it's because of you I decided to get some help. So yes, you played a big role in making me realize I needed to do that."

"I see. I'm glad I was able to help you. So, what are your plans now?"

"Well, I wanted to share some good news with you. I have two job interviews lined up for next week, which I'm really excited about. Both are for project management positions, one at Kaiser Hospital and the other at Salesforce in San Francisco."

"Wow. Look at you. I'm so happy for you. I'm sure you'll land one of them. You're smart and your background is impressive."

"See, that's what I mean. You make me feel like I can do anything."

The waitress returned with their drinks and entree's and placed them on the table.

"There you go. Can I get you anything else?"

They both said, "no thank you," in unison.

"I'm just sayin', you should be proud of yourself. You have the potential to have a great life."

"Thanks so much. Your words mean a lot to me."

"You're welcome."

"By the way. How're things with you and the lucky guy?"

"Uh, a little crazy, but I don't want to talk about that right now."

"I'm sorry to hear that. I hope things work out, kind of," he said, smiling.

Jazmine glanced at her phone to check if Noah had tried to reach her, but he hadn't. Although she'd wanted to enjoy herself and needed a break from the drama, her mind stayed on him. *He normally would've called by now. Why am I even thinking about him? Maybe he's resting.*

Marcus placed his hand on top of hers. "Is everything alright?" he asked.

"Yes, why do you ask?"

"You got a little quiet and seemed distracted about something. I assume he's still in DC right now, otherwise you probably wouldn't be here."

"Yes, he is, but please. We're having a nice time, so let's not ruin it."

"You're right. Did I tell you how beautiful you looked tonight?"

"Yes, you did Marcus."

"Okay, I'm just making sure you heard me. I must admit, I know I'm not in the best position right now, but I'd like to get to know you better. I realize you're not able to spend that much time with me. But I just want you to know I'm here for you, whatever you need."

She'd wanted to tell him; her efforts were only to help him because he needed support, and to explain her sensitivity in helping others, but she held back. Surprised by his comments, she found herself wanting to hear more, which were the exact words she'd needed to hear from Noah. She sat silent staring at him, while trying to control her emotions.

"Everything's going to be alright, Jazmine. I don't know what you're going through, but it must be pretty serious."

"I'm sorry. I don't know what came over me. I might discuss it with you one day."

"No need to say you're sorry. You've been there for me, so I'm here for you, okay?"

"Okay, Marcus."

They continued having small talk while enjoying their dinner. Later, the waitress returned with dessert menus.

"Would either of you like dessert tonight? We have several items on the menu," she asked.

Jazmine glanced over the menu. "They look delicious, but I'll pass. I'll take a cup of ginger white tea though."

"And for you sir?"

"I'll have the same."

"Okay, I'll be right back with your tea," she said, removing their plates.

While drinking their tea, Jazmine had become vulnerable and thought it'd be best to end the evening. Although he'd went out of his way to make her comfortable, the connection between them made her uneasy. When they took a slow walk to her car, he tried to hold her hand, but she pulled it back. The stillness of the night air gave her a sense of relief, as she took a deep breath, trying to release the stress she'd been under.

"Thank you again Jazmine for having dinner with me."

She turned to gaze at him. "You're welcome, I had a good time."

When they'd reached her car, he stopped and stared at her, then pulled her close to him and kissed her. Jazmine didn't hold back, as they caressed each other.

"Marcus, wait we can't do this. Please wait. I have to go."

"Okay, I understand. I'm sorry, but I—"

"No, it's okay. I'll talk with you later."

CHAPTER 17

All Over the Place

The next morning, Jazmine woke up just in time to make it to church service. She hadn't spoken with Erica in a while but needed to get her opinion on an idea she had. After service she waited in the lobby to talk with her.

"Hey there Jazmine, how're you?"

"I'm hanging in there. I'm sorry I haven't been in touch. I'm just all over the place in dealing with you know who."

"Yes, I understand. Are things starting to get better now?"

"No, not at all. I think I'm going to fly out to DC and get a hotel just to see what I can find out. He finally agreed to get some help, but I don't know if I trust what he says anymore."

"That sounds like a good idea. It'll show him how serious you are in trying to work things out."

"Thanks Erica, I'm glad you agree with me. This is really getting old, and he keeps spending our money on gambling."

"I'm so sorry Jazz. I really hope things work out for the both of you."

"Yeah, we'll see."

"By the way, are you still up to being in my wedding or is that too much for you right now?"

"Girl, you know I'm still in. How're the plans going?"

"I actually found a dress I love. I'm considering another one, but I have my heart set on one I saw at The Paris Connection in San Francisco."

"Oh wow, Erica. I'm so happy for you."

"Thank you, Jazz. I'll let you know when I decide on the bridesmaid's dresses."

"Okay, I look forward to it."

"Well, I better get going. My honeybun is waiting in the car for me."

"Okay, I'll keep you updated on my situation. Love you, bye."

"Yes, please do. You hang in there and don't do anything I wouldn't do. Love you too, bye."

A week later, after having inconsistent talks with Noah, she'd made plans to visit DC without letting him know. She wanted to find out if the counseling sessions were helping him and if his gambling had slowed down at all. She hoped this last-ditch effort to save their marriage would help. She'd arranged for a substitute teacher while she focused on trying to work things out in DC. Her mind raced with thoughts of what might happen when she did her investigative work on him. *What if he's in over his head and will just push me away and refuse my help? Or maybe he'll be glad I came to help him because right now we're going nowhere fast.*

Whatever the case, she needed to find out for herself where he stood in his efforts to get better. Before leaving, she'd planned to visit her parents before flying to DC. In most cases, they were able to help in calming her nerves, and she'd hoped it would be the same in this case. She'd made up her mind to do whatever it took to take control of the situation with Noah. For a while she'd isolated herself from her family and friends, and conversations with her parents had gotten shorter because of her fixation in dealing with him.

"Hello?"

"Hi mom, how're you?"

"Hey Jazz, I'm good. How're you? When are you coming by to visit? It's been a while now."

"I know, you're right. I've just been a little busy with work and some other things. I'm sorry I haven't been over to visit in a while. How's dad?"

"He's good. He's missing you too."

"I miss y'all too. Well, I wanted to stop by now if that's okay?"

"Of course, you don't have to ask."

"I know, but I just like to at least let you know that I'm coming by."

"I understand. Just let yourself in. I can't wait to see you."

"Alright, I'll be there shortly."

As she turned the key to enter the house, childhood memories of how her parents use to comfort her flooded her mind. *I'm a grown woman now, and I have to be strong and not let this get the best of me.*

CHAPTER 18

Daddy's Little Girl

Her dad shouted from the kitchen. "Hey Jazmine, is that you?"

"Yes, it's me, dad," she said, while she walked into the kitchen and gave him a hug. "How're you? I'm sorry, I know it's been a while since I've come by, but I've just been dealing with a lot lately."

"I understand. Sometimes life throws us curve balls and we must deal with things the best way we can. You know we're here for you, so you don't have to deal with things on your own. But I know you're stubborn like your mom and try to play super woman. At times I have to remind her we're in this together, sometimes she listens to me and sometimes she doesn't," he said, taking a seat at the kitchen table. "After 35 years of marriage, I've learned to live with it. How's that husband of yours? I'm sure he's back home by now, right? Your energy seems a little low. Are you alright?"

He got right to the point as she gave him a half-smile. He'd suspected her lack of energy had something to do with Noah.

"Yeah, I'm alright dad. And no, he's not back yet. Actually, I'm leaving tomorrow to visit him in Washington."

"Oh wow, they're really keeping him tied to that job. I'm sure you don't like that very much."

"No, I don't dad. He was supposed to be back by now, but they offered him a promotion and he accepted it."

"I see. So, are you going to move there or what are you going to do?"

"Well, supposedly he'll be working from the Vacaville and DC location. So, he'll be traveling and because of covid he'll be working remotely for the most part. Everything's up in the air right now. But it's more than that."

"Oh really. I see."

Her dad's tone expressed concern, while the distraction of her mom walking into the kitchen gave her a welcome relief.

"Hey baby, you made it."

"Yes, I made it Mom," she said, giving her a hug. "I've missed you both."

"Well, we've been here. We didn't want to disturb the newlyweds too much." She smiled and took her hand. "And how's Noah?"

"Noah's okay, I guess. He's still in DC, and I'm going there tomorrow."

"But I thought he was getting a transfer."

"Me too. He's supposed to once he gets adjusted to his new promotion."

"Oh wow, a promotion. Well, good for him. That means you can get your house sooner rather than later and start working on some grandkids."

"I don't know Mom. We're going through some hard knocks right now. That's one reason why I'm flying out there, to see if we can work things out."

"I'm sorry to hear that, Jazmine. I mean...I hope y'all are going to be okay."

"Me too, Mom." Jazmine sighed, trying to restrain her emotions.

"Come on Jazz, it couldn't be that bad, right?"

"I'll see when I get there."

"I remember when your dad went to Texas for a month, and I thought I was going to die. Your grandpa was ill, so he went there to help him out. I felt like I didn't know what to do with myself. I started baking cookies and gained all kinds of weight. I felt a little silly when he got back because time had gone by so fast. So, I'm sure you'll look back at this and realize it wasn't so bad after all."

"Thanks Mom. But this is different. Something's up with Noah and I'm going to get to the bottom of it."

"Wait now. I know how you can be Jazmine. Please don't get out there and get yourself in a bad situation. That's just too far for us to come quick and help you."

"I'll be fine Mom, don't worry."

"Okay, well, let me fix you a plate. It'll all work out, honey. Noah's a good man, and he'd be a fool to let you go."

They sat and ate smothered steak and gravy with mashed potatoes, collard greens and corn bread.

"My goodness Mom, I love this food," Jazmine said, chuckling. "I just can't seem to get my food to taste like yours. I sure miss your cooking."

"Jazz, you know you can come by and have dinner with us any time."

"I know and I'll start coming by more often."

Her dad squinted his eyes, while breaking off a piece of cornbread. "Your gun license is up to date, right?"

"Huh?" Jazmine said.

"Oh James, stop it," her mom said.

"I raised you to know how to protect yourself and I can't be there for you like I use to. He asked you to marry him and he's supposed to look after you. I spoiled your momma and I expect the same for my daughter or he shouldn't have married you."

"Don't worry Dad, I can take care of myself."

"I know you can. You know karate and I taught you how to use that pistol."

"Alright James, that's enough. Leave her alone."

"I'm just sayin', something in my spirit don't feel right. So, if necessary, you take care of yourself, but keep it to yourself. You know what to do."

"James, you're a mess."

"I know dad."

"Baby girl don't pay attention to him. He's always trying to protect you, but I know you'll be alright. You do have a black belt, so I'm not worried. Oops, now here I go," her mom said, chuckling.

"Okay Mom and Dad, I know and I'm good. I'll be fine."

CHAPTER 19

Checking-In

Early Saturday morning, Jazmine checked into the MGM National Harbor Casino Hotel. She'd loved its location in the heart of all the happenings and big enough to avoid being seen. Her faith in their marriage had diminished, but she'd hoped there would still be a chance for them to make it. Noah had promised to keep her updated on his progress, but he'd been acting nonchalant, which didn't sit right with her. Right after she'd finished unpacking, her phone rung.

"Hey Noah."

"Hey baby. What are you up to this morning?"

"I just finished my jog, so I'm just relaxing right now." She remembered the time difference of DC being three hours ahead of California. "What are your plans for today? Did you take your jog this morning?" she asked.

"No, I didn't this time. I had a long busy week, so I stayed in and got some rest."

Although she'd doubted what he said, she didn't bother to question him.

"I hear you, sometimes I feel the same way. But you know me, I like to get my workout in."

"Yes, you're good at staying focused."

"So, you haven't told me much about your counseling program. Do you think this will help you? Tell me more about it?"

"Well, they're pretty reputable, but a little costly. I signed up for the outpatient program which cuts down on costs. And I have the option of going as many times as needed, but for now, I chose to go once a week."

"Once a week? I don't see how that can be effective Noah, but I'm not going to argue with you about it. You know how serious this is and how much it's affecting our relationship. It's all up to you at this point, and I'll do all I can to help you get through this. So, what day of the week did you pick?"

"Thursday. I just figured it would be good to start right before the weekend, which would help me to stay strong through the weekend."

Jazmine shook her head. *Yeah right, you don't just gamble on the weekends. Maybe he'll come to grips with what's happening soon.* "So, what about your job? I know you're still getting adjusted to your new position, but how much longer is this going to take?"

"I don't know for sure Jazmine."

She cut the conversation short before her frustration with him became obvious. His nonchalant attitude had begun to irritate her.

"Alright Noah, I'm going to eat something and jump in the shower. And I need to do a little grocery shopping before meeting with Erica and Sophia for dinner. So, I'll probably be getting in late. If I don't talk with you tonight, I'll call you in the morning."

"Okay, have fun. By the way, how're they doing?"

"Well, Erica is getting married in October, so she's excited about that and Sophia is doing great as well. The real estate business is booming right now, and she's selling houses like crazy. Well, I better get outta here before time gets away from me. I hope you enjoy your day."

"I will, I'm just going to take it easy today. Have fun tonight, Jazz. I love you."

"I love you too, bye."

Jazmine needed to find out how effective his counseling sessions had been. Their bank account showed he'd been making deposits, but they were still a lot less than what they were before. *I don't know if he thinks I'm up to something or not, and*

I can't worry about it right now. She'd changed her clothes and went downstairs to view the lay out of the casino and to find out where the poker tables were located. She spotted a pair of wide-framed glasses in a boutique that went perfect with the burgundy wig she'd brought to disguise herself. She found seating close by the poker tables where she'd planned to sit undetected in her disguised appearance. *He got paid today, so if he's still gambling, tonight would be a good night to catch him in the act. I'm going to see just how much money he spends on gambling.* After she finished browsing and having breakfast, she'd went back to her room and took a nap. Two hours later she received a text message from Marcus.

Marcus: Hi Jazmine, I just wanted to let you know I'm thinking about you and hope you're doing well.

Jazmine: Hi Marcus, I'm doing good. Thank you for thinking about me.

Marcus: Hope I can see you soon. I'm doing good on my new job, and everything is working out well.

Jazmine: That's great to hear. I knew everything would work out.

Marcus: Can we get together soon?

Jazmine: Not right now, but I'll be in touch with you later.

CHAPTER 20

The Poker Table

Jazmine needed to figure out what time Noah would show up at the casino, therefore, she'd planned to call him later to try and gauge when he'd be leaving his apartment. He'd developed a habit of not answering his phone while at the casino, which indicated he might be there or on his way. She called room service to order dinner and waited until close to midnight before heading downstairs. *Checking on him makes me nervous, but it's the only way I know how to deal with this. Doing this will help me to make up my mind on what to do next.* She watched a couple of movies and played games on her phone before getting ready. At 11:00, she started getting dressed—put a few loose curls in her wig and put on a little extra makeup. She pulled out her straight leg black pants, and black balloon sleeved blouse with cut-out shoulders, and slipped on her black 3-inch heels. When she called

Noah, he didn't answer his phone. *This is my cue.* At twelve midnight, she headed down to the casino.

While on the elevator, a group of guys who appeared in their twenties got on when she reached the fourth floor. A couple of them greeted her with a nod, then continued to talk about what happened at a party they'd attended. When the elevator reached the casino floor, she turned the corner, walked past the card tables, and glanced over at the poker table when she spotted Noah. Although his back faced her direction, right away she recognized his body structure. *Look at him, all into it.* She grabbed a seat in the corner of the bar area out of his sight. She'd plan to keep her eyes on him while having a drink and be entertained by the band. The lights were dim in the area where she sat, which made it difficult for anyone to recognize her. The waiter, a slender young man with braids in his hair and a UK accent, approached her table.

"Would you like something to drink?"

"Yes, I'll take a rum and coke please."

"Okay, coming right up."

Oh gosh, I hope I can handle this. She needed to calm her nerves to continue with the task. She observed Noah gambling for an hour, and after drinking three rum and cokes, she wanted to walk around but needed to use the bathroom first. While she combed through her hair, two young ladies were freshening up their make-up. *They're cute, but they look a little on the raunchy side, wearing skimpy outfits.* She smiled and spoke to them, they smiled back but didn't respond.

One of them said, "girl let's go work our magic."

"You know it, let's hit it," the other one said.

Jazmine rolled her eyes and figured they'd planned to try and get money out of a few silly men. On her way back to her seat, she recognized those same two women at the poker table. *What the hell? They better not be having any dealings with my husband.* Confused on how to proceed, she went to get change, then played the slot machines for thirty minutes before heading back to her seat. *What are you going to do now Jazz?* Bored from not having any luck on the slot machines, she walked back over near the poker area. She stopped in her tracks, when she observed a woman rubbing Noah's back while he played poker.

"Who in the hell is that? she said to herself."

She hurried back to the bathroom to calm down, as her heart had started beating faster. *This couldn't be happening. He's really playing me after I've been so patient with him. He's not going to change and he's going to pay for what he's doing to me.* Her hands were shaking while she tried to freshen her make-up. When she returned to her seat, she'd began snapping pictures of them with her phone. She became furious, but she tried to remain calm when the woman placed her hand on the back of his neck as he turned to kiss her. She began having flashbacks about what her dad told her. *'If he wasn't willing to take care of you and spoil you like I did your momma, then he shouldn't have married you.'*

She stood up and grabbed her purse, then reached inside for her gun. "Damn it, I forgot, I left it at home." She headed over to the poker table, and before she got there, the woman had started kissing Noah on his ear as he smiled while sipping his drink. She wanted to grab the woman by her hair and throw her onto the floor.

When she'd reached the poker table, she pushed the woman to the side and said, "really ho, get the hell back."

The woman stumbled backwards and screamed. "Who do you think you are?" She then rushed toward Jazmine, then stopped. "Who are you?" she asked.

Jazmine squinted her eyes and stared at her. "Do you want some of this?"

Noah recognized Jazmine's voice right away and turned around to face her.

"Really Noah. I ought to beat your ass right now. So, you're the big baller and the shot caller, huh Noah, out here playing games with my life?"

She slapped him hard across his face. He gained his composure, then stood there and stared at her and didn't say a word. He understood how upset she'd become and didn't want to make it any worse. He tried to let her calm down, as he'd never seen her that angry before.

"Why are you so quiet? What's wrong now? Drop the damn chips and let's go—now."

Everyone at the poker table stood silent. The man over-seeing the table reached for the security button. "You good man?" he asked.

"Yeah, I'm good," Noah said.

Jazmine let out an evil laugh. "What's wrong— the cat got your tongue? Who is this ho? No, wait don't answer that. So, this is why you won't come back home? You're just having too much fun to consider what you're putting me through, huh?"

CHAPTER 21

What Would My Daddy Do?

Noah had just lost two thousand dollars and had a good hand to win it all back. But because of the scene, he made the choice to listen to Jazmine and avoid even more embarrassment.

"Let's go."

He dropped the chips and asked, "where are we going?"

"Start walking," she demanded.

He gazed at the head poker player.

"I'm good man. Don't call security. This is my wife, I'll be fine."

Jazmine turned around and gazed at everyone at the table, then fixed her eyes on the other woman, staring her up and down. When they got to the elevator, she pushed the button and they headed to the tenth floor with no words spoken. She scanned her card key across the lock to open the door.

"Jazmine, please calm down."

"Oh, now you want me to calm down. I've been calm for a long time, and you've been playing me all this time."

"No, I wasn't playing you."

"Really, explain the whore you were kissing on."

"Oh, she's just a friend."

"I'm not going to let you keep lying to me Noah. You think I'm so dumb and naïve, don't you?"

She slapped him again, then karate kicked him in his stomach.

"Damn, that hurt," he said, rubbing his stomach. "What are you doing? Wait Jazz, I'm sorry. That woman doesn't mean anything to me. It's just something that happens at the poker table."

"Shut up liar!" She picked up a bottle of wine and threw it at him.

He ducked. "Stop, please stop it. You're drunk!"

"Damn it, I missed."

"Jazmine, please stop."

"You thought I was playing. You had no problem embarrassing me."

She grabbed a lamp and threw it at him, grazing his head.

"Have you lost your mind," he said, while blood streamed down his face, he hurried over and grabbed her. "Stop it, just stop it now. You're out of control."

"Whatever, let me go. Unlock your damn phone."

"Please, I'm sorry, I never meant to hurt you."

"Do it now, she said."

"But why?"

"Do it."

He released her. "Okay, hold on. But Jazmine this is ridiculous."

"I'll be the judge of that. Now give it to me."

"Wait Jazmine. I have a friend that I hang out with sometimes, but I don't care about her."

"Oh, is this your friend?" She continued scrolling through pictures of him with other women. "Wait, this one looks like the woman you were kissing on. Look at y'all, at the park, and out having dinner, just enjoying life. And who are these other women. You're pathetic, Noah."

"We're just friends, I promise. We're all at a party and were just snapping pictures."

"I should've brought my damn gun, just so I could've put a bullet in your ass. But you're not worth me going to prison over," she said, while pacing the floor.

"I know I've put you through a lot and I'll make it up to you. With us being separated, it just got the best of me. But I've always loved you. You know that."

"Hm, what would my daddy do?" she said. "You know Noah, I really trusted you. But you just had to take my kindness for granted, didn't you? I never would've thought it would come to this. I had so much hope we'd work things out. Then you started getting back into the gambling scene and now this. Now we are practically broke. I remembered my momma always told me to keep a separate bank account. Good Lord, I'd be homeless if I'd depended on you."

"But I…"

"But I' nothing. You really hurt me this time. Call her right now and put her on speaker. Tell her you don't care about her and that you love me, and you'll never see her again. The crazy part is, I don't even know if I want to be with you anymore. But you're going to pay for what you did to me. Here's the phone, call her right now."

"Okay, okay, I will Jazz… Uh, hello."

"Talk."

"Noah are you alright?" the woman asked.

"Yeah, I just want to let you know I never cared about you, and I love my wife."

"Tell her she means nothing to you," Jazmine said.

"You mean nothing to me and don't ever call me again."

"Now hang up the damn phone."

After hanging up, Noah said, "Jazmine, my head is bleeding, I think I need to go to the hospital."

Exhausted and drained, she flopped down on the bed. "You probably do need to go to the hospital, but right now my head is in a bad place, and that's not good. You're not the same man I married Noah. I'll take you to the hospital in a minute, but first we need to figure out where do we go from here."

"You're getting on my case, but what about you? You tried to hide that you're working with some guy name Marcus, telling me his name is Marsha. What's up with that? I'm not stupid. For all I know you could be seeing him."

"Wait, what? I'm not seeing anyone. I'm only helping him with his issues."

"Who the hell is Marcus anyway."

"I already told you, he's just someone I'm helping who I knew in high school."

"Damn it, Jazmine. Really, well how's that working out? Did you help him find a job? Please, you thought I believed that's what you were doing?"

"Obviously, it's working out fine. I'm here with you right now, trying to find out what the hell is going on with you. And boy, did I get a surprise. Look, Noah don't try to deflect. You're just trying to get off the hook of what you put me through."

"Well, maybe this whole living in different states thing is just too much for us."

"You think? I've been trying to tell you that for the longest."

"Come here Jazz."

"No," she said, trying not to cry. "This is all your fault."

"Please Jazmine, I love you and I don't want us to break up."

"Well, it's too late for that."

"Maybe it's not."

"But I just hit you in the head with a lamp and I'm so exhausted in dealing with you."

"Yeah, you did, but I'll survive. I know I let things get out of hand and I'll do better."

"The only way you can do better is by moving back home right away."

"Well, I think I can move back now, but I'll still have to fly out here from time to time to take care of issues when they arise. You can come back with me as often as you like. I want things to work out between us Jazz, I really do."

"What about your gambling problem?"

"I can get some help in Cali. I'm tired too and I'm ready to come home."

"Are you sure? I mean, we might need some marriage counseling after all of this."

"Jazz, I'll do whatever it takes for us to stay together."

"We'll see, Noah."

CHAPTER 22

Time for Stitches

I'm off for the rest of this week, and it's good that I have this room for two nights because now I need to clean this place up. I figured I'd set you straight about your gambling and we'd work things out. But I never expected to go through any of this. Okay, I'll take you to the hospital, so that you can get checked out. What are you going to say happened to you?" Jazmine asked.

"I got into a fight with someone and was hit in the head."

"Let me look at it. Hm, it doesn't look too bad. It just needs to be cleaned up a little, and you might need a few stitches. Here, take this towel and hold it to your head while I change clothes and put a cap on. I really made a mess in here and I know I'll be charged big time for it. But I'll come back later to try and clean up what I can."

"You'll definitely have to pay for this mess."

"Shut up Noah. I'm glad I parked in the parking lot, so when we get downstairs, let's go out the backway. Plus, I don't want to walk through the casino."

"Neither do I."

Jazmine waited in the car for two hours before his release from the hospital.

"I'm done. They said it could've been worse, but they cleaned it up and put six stitches in my head and told me to take ibuprofen if I need to."

"Well, I'm kind of sorry. I was completely out of control. I know I had too much to drink, and I lost it. But you put me in that situation, so I blame you for letting this happen."

"I know, I know. Let's go to my apartment. I need to lie down."

"Me too. I'm exhausted."

He'd taken an emergency week off from work, which they'd spent getting rid of items he no longer needed. They donated most of his furniture and the following week they'd flew back home to California. Shortly after moving back, he began working out of the Vacaville location. She didn't hesitate in setting up a counseling program for him, to prevent a delay in getting help with his gambling addiction. She also arranged for them to begin marriage counseling at the church she'd attended.

A few weeks later, Jazmine took part in Erica's wedding, and they had a great time celebrating with them. During marriage counseling, they made a promise to be there for each other and to never take each other for granted again. They began to live their life the way she'd wanted, and their bank account had started to grow again. She made it a point to text Marcus, letting him know about her reconciliation with Noah and that she'd no longer be in contact with him. She wished him all the best in his life, but he didn't respond. At times, he crossed her mind, and she hoped his life had changed for the better. Although she wanted to check on him, she'd tried to remain focused on keeping her marriage together.

Later, Noah needed to fly to DC to meet with his subordinates and to discuss upcoming projects with his colleagues. Jazmine chose not to join him and looked forward to spending time to herself. She wanted to use that time, to gain her sense of identity back because she'd began to lose confidence in herself and had started second guessing everything. She needed to clear her mind and questioned whether to sacrifice her sanity, just to have a house, and live with a man she no longer treasured. He assured her he'd only be there for one week, but she doubted he'd be there just for business. They embraced before parting at the Oakland Airport and gave each other a quick peck on the lips. Noah wanted to leave her with a kiss she'd remember, but he followed her lead. He understood, even though they had gone through counseling, her attitude toward him had changed. When she dropped him off, she got in the car and turned her music up loud and began singing. She loved pop music, while Noah preferred listening to jazz, which had begun to get on her nerves. In fact, everything about him had started getting on her nerves. She'd spoken with Erica earlier in the week and they'd planned a hiking trip at the Sequoia Bayview Trail. She wanted to use that time to share her thoughts with Erica and to enjoy her freedom.

"These trees are so majestic and beautiful. I really needed this. The air is fresh, and it feels so good to be on my own for a while," Jazmine said.

"Yes, they're awesome. It's too bad some of them have been burned by the fire. So, how're things going with you and Noah? Are things better now?"

"Yes and no. I mean, I don't even know if I want to continue in this relationship. It would've been better if Noah had decided to come home on his own. But it took me catching him in the act for him to make that decision and putting a gash in his head for him to wake up. I just don't know... On the other hand, Marcus treats me like someone special, and it reminds me that I deserve to be treated better than how Noah has been treating me. I know how you feel about the sanctity of marriage, but Noah isn't the man I thought he was, so I might have to make a decision."

"I understand, sometimes we jump into relationships just for the sake of being with someone without weighing everything involved. Yes, I do believe in doing all you can to work things out before throwing in the towel. So, take your time and let's keep it in prayer."

"I'll continue to pray, but if he does one more thing to hurt me, I'm done. And I can't worry about what others may think about me. I mean, I've been doing all I can to hang in there and I don't like to fail at anything, but I can only take so much."

CHAPTER 23

The Car Accident

Two days later Jazmine received a call from Noah.

"Hey Noah."

"Hey how's it going? Um, I'm calling to let you know that I was in a car accident. I'm okay though, but I wanted to let you know."

"What...what do you mean? Are you okay?"

"Yeah, I am."

"Are you at the hotel?"

"Uh, no. I'm in the hospital."

"What...oh my gosh Noah, you must be hurt pretty bad for you to be in the hospital. I'm catching the next flight out. What hospital are you in?"

"Um, I'm at George Washington Hospital. But you don't really need to come, Jazz. I'm sure I'll be outta here in no time."

"What are you talking about Noah? What's your room number?"

"Room 304, on the 3rd floor."

"I'm going to call the airline right now to make reservations. I'll stay in your room at the hotel. So, I'll call you back to let you know what time my flight leaves."

"Thanks Jazz. I love you."

"I love you too."

Jazmine took a red eye flight to DC and arrived at the hospital early the next morning. She packed light because she'd wanted to go straight to the hospital. She became nervous and uneasy about the accident and wasn't able to rest on the plane. She remembered having panic attacks when visiting her dad in the hospital last year. His heart attack had pushed her over the edge, and she didn't want to experience that again. On the way to his room, she'd tried to remain positive and not focus on the gloomy expressions on the faces of people she passed. *I hope he's going to be okay. I'm glad he sounded good on the phone.*

"Hey Jazz, you made it."

With tears in her eyes, she kissed his forehead. "Yes, I did. How're you feeling? You don't look good."

"I'm fine. Just a little sore."

"Wow, Noah I don't like seeing you like this. How did this happen?"

"Well, I was exiting the freeway heading towards Columbus and Main, when another car merged into my lane from my right side, coming from the other off ramp. I didn't even see him until it was too late. I wanted to move, but I had nowhere to go, so when he hit me, my car flipped over. That scared the hell out of me. Thank goodness people pulled over to help me. I couldn't reach my phone to call for help, but I'm glad someone called the ambulance and the police. It was a mess."

"My goodness Noah. I'm so glad you're okay, but you're not looking too good right now. Did you even see who it was that hit you?"

"Yeah, I did, he was some young dude who had too much to drink, and apparently he didn't even come out with a scratch on him. They did some X-rays last night and said I have a few fractured ribs and my left leg is broken, which I may need to have pins put in."

"Gosh Noah. I bet you're hurting pretty bad."

"I am, but they gave me some strong pain medication, so I don't feel too much."

"Wow, I bet you were scared to death. I can't even imagine."

"Yeah, it was pretty scary. He hit me hard."

"Try not to think about it too much right now. Just relax and get some rest. We can talk about it more later."

She sat next to his bed and held his hand for an hour while he slept, then went to the cafeteria to grab a cup of coffee. When she returned, his doctor came in to examine him.

"Good morning, Mr. Wright. How're you feeling?"

"I've been better."

"Good morning doctor," Jazmine said.

"Hello, I'm Dr. Lawrence. And you are?"

"I'm his wife, Jazmine."

"It's nice to meet you. He'll need lots of rest and he's scheduled to have surgery on his leg tomorrow morning."

"Yes, he told me. He mentioned he may need to have pins put in his leg."

"Yes, based on the x-ray, it looks that way. It'll help to stabilize his leg while it heals."

"So, can that make it take longer to heal?"

"It depends, not necessarily, but they are used to hold things in place while the body heals. So, he'll need to take it easy for a while."

"I understand."

"I'm sorry to bother you Mr. Wright, but I need to examine you for a few minutes prior to you having surgery. It might hurt a little, so I hope the pain meds have kicked in by now."

"Me too. I just can't believe what happened," Noah said.

"I understand. Accidents happen fast when we least expect it. I'll try to be quick, so that you two can spend some time together."

"Thanks doc."

Jazmine cringed while watching the doctor examine Noah.

"I'm sorry Mr. Wright, unfortunately you'll be in pain for some time. But eventually the pain will lessen as you begin to heal. Alright, I'm all done now."

"Yeah, that wasn't fun. But thanks doc," Noah said.

A few minutes later, his lunch arrived.

"Here you go Mr. Wright. Enjoy your lunch."

"Thank you."

Jazmine got up to open the top on his plate. "Let's see what we have here. Hm, not bad. They brought you a grilled chicken sandwich with a green salad. It doesn't look bad for hospital food. Baby, do you feel like eating a little something?"

"Yes, I do, but I'm not sure if I can feed myself."

"Don't worry, that's what I'm here for. Let me break this up for you."

While she prepared his food, his face expressed concern, but she assumed it had to do with his injuries.

"Take your time baby, you got this."

He began to feed himself, but after a while he became tired, then she took over and fed him.

"Was there an exchange of information with the other driver taken by the police?" she asked.

"Yes, it was."

"Good. I'll call the insurance company tomorrow to make sure they have all the information they need to get things going."

"Don't worry Jazz. I'll take care of it."

"Really Noah, and how do you plan to do that. You can barely feed yourself. Don't worry I'll handle it. Do you think you've had enough to eat?"

"Yeah, I'm good. But I do need to use the bathroom."

"Uh oh, you better hit the light to call for a nurse. When they come in to help you, I'm going downstairs to grab a bite to eat. Do you want me to call your mom to let her know about the accident?"

"No, please, not right now. I'll contact her later."

"Alright, but I know she'll try to blame me for not letting her know sooner."

"Don't worry, I'll handle her."

"If you say so."

Jazmine found a place under a shade tree to relax while eating her lunch. She sat and reflected on all she and Noah had been through up until now. *Wow, this is crazy. I'm so thankful he's okay. Things are not perfect between us, but I can't imagine giving up now.* She wanted to show her love by being there for him and hoped that would help to bring them closer. A speedy recovery is what she'd wished for, but understood it was going to take time. After taking another sip of her coke, she headed back to his room. As she got closer to his room, she overheard a woman walking in front of her talking on the phone.

"I'm going to visit Sandra because she was in a car accident last night and the car flipped over," the woman said.

CHAPTER 24

After the Surgery

While Noah laid asleep in bed, Jazmine sat staring at him recalling what she'd overheard the lady say about the accident. She tried to convince herself the lady had to be talking about someone else. She wanted to wake him up to ask him about it, but she didn't bother. Thirty minutes later he opened his eyes.

"Hey, I'm sorry I keep falling asleep on you."

"No problem. You need your rest. Plus, you're on some pretty strong meds, so you'll be constantly falling asleep. What time are you scheduled for surgery in the morning?"

"They said, 7:00 am from what I remember."

"Okay, I'll be here when you get out."

"Thank you, Jazz, for coming. I'm really glad you're here."

"Where else would I be," she said, smiling. "Are you nervous?"

"Not really, for some reason."

"Good. You'll be fine."

That would've been a perfect time to ask him more about the accident. But she didn't want to risk starting an argument and getting him upset the day before his surgery. Plus, she wanted him to tell her on his own.

"I need to get your hotel card key, so that I can take my luggage to your room."

"It's in my wallet. Let me call the nurse to bring my wallet because they put it away for safety reasons."

"I also want to freshen up a bit. Then I'll be back in a few hours to help you with dinner."

After the nurse returned his wallet, Jazmine gave him a kiss before leaving. When she got to his hotel room, she'd fell back on the bed, exhausted from the over-night flight and from finding Noah in pain. She laid there staring at the ceiling, trying to imagine how long she'd have to stay in DC and how soon he'd be able to come home. After unpacking and hanging up her clothes, she called her parents.

"Hey Mom and Dad , I'm sure you're probably out shopping. But I wanted to let you know I flew out to DC overnight because Noah was in a car accident. He's doing okay but is having surgery in the morning on his leg. I'm staying at the Embassy Suites right now, and I'll keep you posted on how everything goes, love you."

She took a much-needed nap after her shower and woke up to a text message from Marcus.

Marcus: Hey Jazmine, I just wanted to say hi and I hope you're doing well. In case you're wondering, things are going good on my end. Miss your smile.

She made several attempts to reply to his text message but kept deleting them. Then chose to respond later and got dressed to head back to the hospital. Because she wanted to brighten Noah's day, she'd stopped to pick up a bouquet of colorful flowers at a florist outside the hospital. By the time she made it back to his room, they'd dropped off his dinner.

"Hey there, I'm back. Looks like I made it just in time to help you with dinner."

"Hey baby, you look refreshed. Wow, you brought me some flowers."

"Yes, I did. I just wanted to try and brighten up your day. I'll just sit them on this table. I also took a nap, so I'm feeling better."

"Thanks baby, that's so sweet of you. And I'm glad you got some rest. I don't want you to wear yourself out worrying about me."

"You're welcome. I'm good though. How're you feeling?"

"The same, just looking forward to getting out of here."

"I know you are, but you have to be patient. It'll happen." Let's see what they brought you for dinner. She lifted the top off his plate. Hm, it looks good, there's mash potatoes and gravy with green beans and baked chicken, and you have chocolate cake for dessert."

"It smells good, so we'll see what it tastes like," he said.

"We can always add some salt and pepper since you're not on a strict diet like some patients are."

"You're right about that, thank goodness."

After she finished helping to feed him, she'd stayed for a couple of more hours, then left because of his scheduled surgery the next morning. She had a restless night sleep because of her concern about his surgery, and what she'd over-heard the lady say on the phone. The next morning, she arrived early to the hospital. She tried waiting in his room for him to come out of recovery. But because of her anxiety, she went to find a nurse.

"Good morning, I'm wondering how my husband is doing. He had surgery this morning. His name is Noah Wright."

"Let me check... Oh yes, he's still in recovery," the nurse said.

"I see, do you have any idea how much longer he'll be there?"

"They should be bringing him out shortly, but I'll check for you."

"Thank you."

"Oh, it looks like they're rolling him out now."

The anesthesia hadn't quite worn off when they rolled him out of recovery.

"Good morning baby," Jazmine said.

"Hey good morning, you're here early."

"Yes, I am."

Jazmine sat quiet while the nurses moved him back onto his bed.

"Try to get some rest Mr. Wright. The doctor will be in to check on you sometime this morning," the nurse said.

Jazmine glanced at her phone when it rung, but she didn't answer it.

"How're you feeling?"

"I'm okay, just a little drowsy but not bad. I'm sure I'll be starting physical therapy soon, because they want me to stay as active as I can."

"That's going to hurt some, but it'll get better with time. By the way, your mom just called and left a message on my phone. She never calls this early, and she sounded worried. I assume you haven't told her what happened. Are you planning on calling her soon?"

"Yeah, I will."

"Alright, well, I'm going to run down to the cafeteria to get a cup of coffee. I just wanted to check on you first."

When she returned to his room, she'd found a gentleman there who had a strange expression on his face.

"Hello," she said.

"Hello, you must be Jazmine. My name is Jamal. It's nice to meet you."

"Yes, I am. It's nice to meet you as well."

"Baby, Jamal is one of my co-workers. He just stopped by to visit me. Thank you, man, I appreciate you checking on me. Let everyone on the job know I'll be outta here soon."

"Sure, no problem. You get some rest and I'll be in touch. Again, it was nice meeting you Jazmine."

"You as well, Jamal. Take care."

"That was nice of him to stop by, and he came so early. I was a little surprised he knew my name."

"It's because I have your picture on my desk, and when we got married, I shared a few pictures with some of my coworkers."

"Oh okay," she said, smiling. "He seemed a little off, as if he was upset about something."

"You think so. He didn't seem upset to me."

CHAPTER 25

Noah's Text Messages

That afternoon, Noah's mom called again. "Noah, I'm about ready to take this call from your mom. You can't just keep avoiding her."

"No, wait."

"Hi Mom. How're you? Yes, I understand. I'll let you talk with him."

Noah shook his head, then took the phone. "Hey Mom, how're you doing? I know, and I'm sorry I haven't returned your calls... I was in a car accident the other day, but I'm fine... Yes, I know Mom, I should've called you, but I just didn't want you to get upset. I had surgery on my leg this morning and it went well, so I don't want you to worry. I should be out of here in a few days."

Jazmine listened while Noah tried to explain why he hadn't returned her calls. He then handed her the phone. She waved her hand and whispered, "no," before taking the phone. His mom's voice began to crack as she scolded Jazmine for not letting her know he'd been in an accident. Jazmine tried being patient with her and remained quiet while letting her vent. She didn't want to say something she might regret.

"Yes, I understand. I know you're upset, and I tried to get him to call you to let you know what happened. He's doing good though, and his surgery went well, so he should be out of here soon. Uh-huh, uh-huh… Okay Mom. I'll be sure to keep you updated on how he's doing, and I'll give you a call back later, alright? Okay, good-bye."

"Don't let her bother you, Jazz. She's too controlling."

"You can say that again. I'm not trying to deal with all of that. There's something I need to talk with you about. But I'm trying to give you a chance to get some rest."

"Hm, did something happen?"

"No, I just need to clarify some information, but I'll wait until you get your strength back."

"Alright. Well, I am a little out of it."

The next day, she remembered to charge Noah's phone. While he slept, she plugged it in and discovered several unread text messages. *Wow, he has a lot of unread text messages on here.*

Jamal: Man, I need my thirty thousand dollars and I'm tired of waiting...

David: Where's my damn money, Noah...

Jamal: I heard about the accident you were in, and I'll be up there...

Sandra: Hey, I was released from the hospital, now how're we...

Lisa: Call me back so we can figure out how to get...

Mom: Noah, I've been trying to reach you, call me back. I'm worried...

Jazmine didn't want to believe what she'd just read. *What is this all about? I'm definitely getting my questions answered today.* Her suspicion about Jamal's visit had been exposed. Noah had lied about why Jamal came to visit him and didn't want to tell her about the money he owed him. He not only owed Jamal money, but because of his gambling debts, he'd owed others money as well.

"Hey baby, I didn't hear you come in. How long have you been here?"

"For only a few minutes. Just long enough to find out you haven't changed."

"What do you mean?"

"So, you owe Jamal thirty thousand dollars?"

"What?"

"Don't 'what' me Noah, just answer the question."

His eyes locked with hers. "To be honest when I was heavy into gambling, I borrowed some money from him. But I'm going to pay him back."

"Well, apparently, he's tired of waiting. So where do you expect to get that kind of money from? And about the accident...was there someone else in the car with you?"

"Huh?"

"Do you want me to repeat the question? Who was it this time Noah? You out here ballin' spending all kinds of money and acting like you're some damn Romeo or something."

"Oh, it was a friend, she had car problems and just needed a ride to—"

"Stop, just stop, it's always a friend. You know what—I'm done with you. I've been trying my best to work things out, but you keep going backwards. Why didn't you tell me about all of this? I had to find out from reading all those damn text messages."

"I'm sorry Jazz, I was going to tell you everything, but I knew you'd be upset."

"Upset, really. I'm past upset. I don't even care anymore Noah. I've become numb to you and your lies. You know, if it wasn't for my friend Erica, I would've left your ass a long time ago. You took my kindness for granted. Well, I hope you enjoy the mess you've gotten yourself into. Maybe one day you'll get yourself together before you lose everything. I'm going to head back home to try and figure out what to do with my life."

He tried raising up in bed to reach for her. "Wait Jazmine. Please don't leave me."

"You better respond to your urgent messages especially the ones asking about their money. They sound tired just like I am. Here's your damn phone."

She threw it at him, hitting his leg.

"Ouch! Jazz...please...please forgive me?"

She grabbed her purse and put her hand out, while walking backwards toward the door.

"Enough Noah. I've had enough. I forgave you a long time ago, but it's time for me to do what's best for me now. Good-bye Noah."

The next morning, she took the first flight back to California. Before heading home, she stopped by Bank of America to withdraw all the money in their joint account, then drove to Chase Bank to deposit it into hers. She considered it a mission to start her life over without him. Her phone showed five missed calls from him which she refused to answer. *I told you I'm done with you, so leave me the hell alone.* She tried to remain calm, but tears continued to roll down her face while unpacking her clothes. She resented him for all she'd found out and concluded he had no plans to change. After spending hours of struggling to accept what had happened, she reached out to the only friend she trusted.

"Hey Erica, it's me. How's it going?"

"It's fine, how're you? You sound down."

"I'm hanging in there. I just got back from DC. Noah was in a car accident, so I went there to be with him."

"Oh no, I'm so sorry to hear that, Jazz. Is he alright?"

"Yes, he is, but he broke his left leg, and fractured his ribs. He had surgery the other day. At any rate, I've decided I'm done with him. So, I just wanted to let you know."

"Wait, huh? But he's still in the hospital, right?"

"Yep, that's where he was when I left him. But you have to understand, I found out by mistake that he owes this guy thirty-thousand dollars he borrowed for gambling. And he owes money to other people as well. Not to mention he was with another woman, who he said was a so-called friend, at the time of the accident. I've tried to deal with him, but he just keeps taking me on this crazy merry-go-round and I'm ready to get off the ride. I understand, no marriage is perfect, but it takes two to make it work and I feel like I'm in this by myself. Who knows what else that fool is into? I feel like an emotional wreck right now."

"I'm sorry Jazz. I understand. You sure have given it your all, so do what you need to do to keep your sanity."

"Thanks Erica. I appreciate your support."

"You know I'm here for you Jazz, and… I just want you to be okay. So, let's get together soon."

"I know, and I'll be in touch. Love you."

"I love you too."

CHAPTER 26

A Fresh Start

Although hesitant about moving on with her life, one month later, Jazmine filed for a legal separation. She hoped that one day Noah would change but refused to keep waiting around for it to happen. He'd stopped by last week to get his clothes, limping with a cane from the effects of the accident. She had concerns about his well-being and prayed for him in hopes he'd get it together before something worse happened to him. She continued her jogging routine passed Starbucks, and at times wondered if Marcus was inside. When time allowed, he'd sit and have coffee, hoping to catch a glimpse of her jogging by. She tried to ignore her desire to check on him but gave him a call one morning when she'd finished her jog.

"Hey Marcus, how're you?"

"Oh wow, Jazmine, I'm doing great. How're you? It's so nice to hear your voice."

"I'm doing good. It's nice to hear your voice as well."

She smiled upon hearing the excitement in his voice. Right away he began updating her on how well his life had changed for the better.

"I'm sorry. I know I'm talking my head off. It's just so nice to hear from you."

"It's fine," she said, chuckling. "I know, it's been a while since we've talked."

"So, how're things going with you? Is everything better now? I mean, I haven't heard from you in a while, so I figured things were going well."

She hesitated because she hadn't prepared on how to respond to his questions.

"Um, yes…things are better. It was a little crazy for a while, so let's just say I'm taking a break and living my life for me now. I'm considering going back to school to finish my education in psychology, which is a dream of mine. Helping people have always been in my DNA, so that's where my head is right now. I actually feel like I have a fresh start."

"A fresh start. I like how that sounds. You should definitely follow your dreams. I can see you now, having your own practice. And I'd be right there to support you. If possible, I'd love to have lunch one day."

"Yes, that might be possible," she said, smiling.

"I'm so glad you called. I really miss spending time with you. And I'm sure you're busy, but I hope you can take a little break sometime soon and meet me for a bite to eat. Let me know when you're free, and I'll make arrangements to get together."

"Okay I will. Talk with you later."

"Good-bye, Jazmine."

That evening she enrolled in U.C. Berkeley to continue working toward her degree in psychology. Her decision to go back to school helped to increase her confidence and sense of identity. Teaching and studying had filled most of her time, and at that point, she was at peace. Noah had moved into his own apartment and continued his counseling sessions for his gambling addiction. Because she still had access to their bank account, she found he'd started back making his regular deposits. One month later she received a call from him.

"Hi Noah."

"Hey Jazz. I was just thinking about you and wanted to hear your voice. How're you?"

"I'm good. Just trying to stay on top of my studies. How're you?'

"I'm hanging in there. Is it possible I can see you soon?"

"Um...I guess so."

"Can I stop by for a while on Saturday, maybe at 1:00?"

"Sure."

All week Jazmine had anxiety about meeting with him. She tried to figure out why he wanted to visit her. *I wonder if he's ready to move forward with getting a divorce.* Saturday morning, he called her to confirm his visit. At 12:45, her doorbell rang.

"Oh gosh, he's a little early. Let me dab on some lip gloss."

When she opened the door, he stood there with one hand behind his back.

"Hey Noah, come on in. What are you hiding?"

He presented her with a bouquet of pink roses in a crystal vase.

"Oh my, I didn't expect this. Wow, they're beautiful." She smiled while placing them on her coffee table.

"I just wanted to give you something special. I know material things don't take the place of the basic needs that make a relationship work, but I figured I'd start somewhere. I hope you like them."

"Yes, I do. But you didn't have to do that. We'll get through this. I mean... it's been a learning experience for both of us."

"How're your studies going? I'm sure it's been hard to keep up with your responsibilities as a teacher and taking classes online."

"Yes, it can be challenging, but I'm determined to get through this."

"You've always been the stronger one between us. And I've always admired that about you even though I never told you."

"It may appear that way, but I struggle just like everyone else. So, what did you want to see me about?"

"Well, I just thought maybe we can work on getting back together. I know I hurt you Jazz and I now realize how selfish I've been. You're the best thing that ever happen to me, and I understand if you're not interested, but I hope you at least think about it. In case you're wondering, I'm still attending the counseling sessions for the gambling issues I had."

"Uh...I didn't expect this, Noah. I mean, it hasn't even been that long since we separated. Every time I replay all that I went through I get upset. I just don't know right now. Counseling didn't even help us, so how can we expect to make it work. I'm glad you're taking your counseling sessions serious though."

"Okay, I'm not going to keep you. I'm sure you have a lot of things to do. I just wanted to see you and let you know what I've been thinking."

Jazmine's new puppy woke up from his nap and came over and sat next to her.

"A French poodle. When did you get this little one?"

"About a week ago. I needed some company," Jazmine said, picking him up. "He's been a big help to me."

"Good for you, Jazz. I'm happy for you. I'm going to head out now. Please think about what we discussed. We can talk more about it later."

"Alright, I will. Thank you for the flowers."

"You're welcome. Take care."

After he left, she sat on her couch and held her puppy. "That crazy man, what makes him think I want to be bothered with him again. He did look good though," she said to herself. "Come on, let me feed you, so I can get back to work."

The following Saturday, she met Erica and Sophia for dinner at Scott's Seafood in Jack London Square. After she took a sip of her drink, she'd spotted Noah and his family sitting at a table across the room. Right away she put her drink down and cleared her throat when she'd made eye contact with his mom.

"My goodness. There's Noah sitting over there with his mom and sister. I guess I should go over and speak to them."

"Uh oh," Erica said.

"Yeah, it's best for you to go over there to speak, instead of him coming over here and you just wave at them. That'll just give her something to talk about," Sophia said.

"She acts like she's not happy to see me, but I'll go over to greet them anyway."

Jazmine took another sip of her drink, then strolled over to their table.

"Hey everyone, what a nice surprise to see you all. Hi mom," she said, while she bent down to press her cheek against hers.

"It's a surprise to see you too," his mom said.

"Oh wow, Jazmine, I didn't realize you were here," Noah said, standing up to give her a hug.

"I know, I didn't realize you all were here either. I'm having dinner with Erica and Sophia."

"Oh, okay, I just thought I'd treat Mom and Monique to dinner."

Jazmine went over and touched Monique on her shoulder.

"Hey there Monique, how're you?"

"I'm good, now that my brother's back."

"I know what you mean. I'm sure you're happy he moved back to California."

"Yep, and we have lots of plans too, right Noah."

"Yeah, but remember I also have to work," he said, chuckling.

"Well, I'll let you all continue your dinner. I'm gonna head back to my table now."

"Okay, Jazz, I'll talk with you later," Noah said, while his sister rolled her eyes.

"Alright, good-bye everyone, enjoy your dinner."

Jazmine plopped down on her seat when she got back to her table.

"Man, that was awkward. It just doesn't seem real, how Noah and I aren't together anymore. I know they're happy to have him back in their lives. It's cool though. He's a momma's boy anyway."

"Well sis, you never know, maybe you two will get back together later. You just never know," Erica said.

"Maybe...who knows."

CHAPTER 27

Two Offers

Jazmine's spirits were low after coming across Noah and his family at the restaurant. *Well, they got him back, and I'm sure they're happy now.* When she got home, she slid open her patio door to catch a breeze from the night air. She popped in a jazz CD by Kirk Whalum that Noah had left behind. She sat on the couch and gazed at her roses as a few more of them had opened, then picked up her puppy and stretched out on the couch while he cuddled next to her.

"Hey there, what are you up to? Looks like it's just going to be me and you on this new journey." *Wow, I'm listening to jazz. That's different. Damn, I miss him, I think.*

That next week she struggled to focus on her studies. She tried not to think about how she wished things would've turned out different with her and Noah. Overwhelmed with her student's assignments and homework, she skipped jogging that week. Friday morning before leaving for work, she received a call from him.

"Hey Noah?"

"Hey baby, I miss you. I'm sorry, I can't do this." His voice was cracking. "Jazz, you mean the world to me, and I can't stop thinking about you."

"Uh, I really wanted things to be right between us, Noah, and we had so many plans, but now things are different."

"I know Jazz, but we can make it work. I promise you I'll be the man you want me to be. Please give me another chance to make it work. I mean can I at least take you out sometimes. We can date for a while to see how things go, then let's see what happens, but I have to see you, Jazz. Can I take you out tomorrow night? We can go wherever you want to go."

"Let me think about it. I...I'll call you tomorrow, alright?"

"Okay, Jazz, I love you."

"Okay."

She tossed and turned that night, before falling asleep around 2:00 am. *I must be strong. Maybe going out with him one time will help me to figure out what I want to do, because Lord knows I don't.* The next morning, after eating breakfast she began doing her homework. After studying for a couple of hours, she'd began to nod. She took a long nap and woke up to a text message from Marcus.

Marcus: Hey Jazmine. How're you? I'm sure you've been busy with homework and teaching. It's been a while since we've talked.

Jazmine: Hey there, I'm doing good. Thanks for checking on me. Yes, I've been pretty busy. This is a bigger challenge than I expected. But it'll all be worth it in the end.

Marcus: I'd like to take you out tonight if you can get away. I'm sure you can use a break.

Jazmine: Yes, I can use a break. But let me think about it. I'll get back with you shortly.

Marcus: Okay.

While soaking in the tub, she'd tried to figure out if she should give Noah another chance or just live her life on her own. She accepted that Marcus wanted to be in a relationship, but because of the reeling affects and drama she'd gone through with Noah, she wanted to enjoy her life in peace. She had mixed feelings about her relationship with Noah because she'd become afraid to trust him again. Teaching and working toward getting her degree were draining her and she needed to find a way to control her anxiety. She chose to decline both offers for dinner because she just wanted to relax. She first sent a text to Marcus.

Jazmine: Hey Marcus, I know we haven't gotten together in a while, and I'm sorry, but I'm tired and I've got a lot of studying to do. Let's get together another time.

Marcus: Sure Jazmine, hopefully we can get together soon.

She then sent a text to Noah.

Jazmine: Hey Noah, I'm tired and I have a lot of studying to do, so I'm going to stay in tonight. Thanks for the offer.

Noah: I understand, maybe I can just come over for a while. I promise to keep quiet. I can even bring over some food, so you don't have to cook.

Jazmine smiled and was taken aback by his reply. She wanted to say no, but she liked his offer to bring her something to eat. He knew how she preferred peace and quiet while studying and use to enjoy taking breaks to cuddle with him.

Jazmine: Okay, but you must be quiet. I mean, you can watch TV, but keep the volume turned down low.

Noah: I know the rules. I'll be there around 6:00.

Jazmine: Okay.

She loved being in control of her life and not have to depend on anyone else. She believed Noah in wanting to start over, but if she'd chose to go that route, he'd have to do it her way.

When he rang the doorbell at 6:00. She opened the door and smiled.

"Hi Noah, come on in."

"Hey Jazz, how's it going?"

"It's fine. I needed a break, so you came just in time. What have you got there?"

"I brought your favorite Chinese food."

"Yum. I'm hungry too."

"Me too, so let's eat."

He dished the food out onto the plates as they prepared to eat.

"Here you go Jazz," he said, sitting her plate in front of her.

"Thank you."

He took her hand and said, "Let me first give thanks for the food."

"Sure."

She loved how they were enjoying each other's company without any issues.

"So, Jazz, I don't know if you heard, but there are some beautiful homes being built in Hayward. I drove over to look at them. They're really nice."

"No, I didn't know that. I'm sure they're beautiful. Are there any schools close by?"

"Yes, there's an elementary school in the area and another one is being built along with a boys and girls club."

Jazmine didn't want to appear as if she wasn't interested. But mentally, she'd moved on with her life and looked forward to new endeavors.

"Sounds nice. This food is so good. It's just what I needed."

"I'm glad I brought it over."

During dinner they had light conversation. She avoided talking about their relationship or anything serious because she'd already had enough going on. When they'd finished eating, she headed back to her bedroom to study. Noah occupied his time by watching a movie and replying to emails from work. After a couple of hours of studying, she came out and sat on the couch next to him.

"Thank you again for bringing the chinese food. I really appreciate it."

"No problem, I know how hard it is to stay focused, and it's easy for eating to be put on the back burner. So, I want you to keep your strength up."

"You were right, my mind was nowhere near food, so that was perfect timing. I don't want you to sit here bored, and I'm sure you're probably ready to go home now." *Wow, that sounded weird. This was his home, before we broke up.*

"I'm fine. How's your studying going?"

"It's a lot, but I'm just trying to keep from getting too overwhelmed."

"I hear you. Well, maybe I should go, so you can get some rest."

"Yes, I'm tired."

"Can I call you tomorrow?"

"Sure."

He held her hand as they walked toward the door.

"Get some rest, Jazz, and don't stay up too late."

"No, I'm good. I'll be hitting the pillow early tonight. I'm already exhausted."

He reached his arms out to give her a hug.

"Hmm, that looks dangerous."

"Okay Jazz, I hear you. Maybe next time," he said, smiling.

"Goodnight, Noah."

"Goodnight, Jazz." He stood outside her door and gazed at her before walking away.

CHAPTER 28

Upcoming Finals

Jazmine had to prepare for upcoming finals, therefore, she avoided all outside activities that interfered with her focus. Just like everything else she'd strived for in life, doing her best to achieve her goals were her strongest desire, even if that meant she had to go at it alone.

The following week, she arranged to meet with Erica for dinner on Friday at the Berkeley Boathouse because she'd wanted to celebrate her accomplishment in passing her classes. During dinner they made a toast to her achievement, but Erica had concern about her lack of enthusiasm because her level of excitement appeared low.

"Hey sis, is everything okay?"

"Yeah, I'm just enjoying this food. Sorry if I'm being quieter than normal. Teaching and finding time to study have been so overwhelming. I really needed to take a break."

"I'm sure. I don't know how you do it."

"Much prayer, much power."

"Yes, that's the truth," Erica said, smiling.

"It gets tough though. But I'm not giving up."

"So, what are your plans about you and Noah?"

"What do you mean?"

"Well, do you plan to stay separated for a while?"

"I'm not sure exactly what to do. He says he wants to get back together, but I have so much peace right now. I don't want to take a chance and get back into that drama."

"Do you think he's changed and want to do right by you?"

"I guess. Then there's Marcus. He's so different from Noah. Which is good, of course. I mean I feel so relaxed around him now that he's gotten his life together. I feel like I went through a whirlwind with Noah. I'm sure issues will arise with Marcus, but right now he gives me the space I need with no pressure at all. He's just so easy going, and he respects me. I feel like that's just what I need right now, no pressure. In a way, I still care about Noah, but I don't like him. Although I feel comfortable when I'm with him, I just don't want to settle."

"I see. You know there's a marriage retreat coming up at the church, maybe you and Noah should go."

"I don't know about that. He came by the other night while I studied, which is fine, but I'm hesitant to put all my trust in him again. He was just so inconsiderate of my feelings about things. But I do need to make up my mind. Either way, I'm not going to rush into anything."

"Well, you have a couple of months to think about it. But the tickets do sale out fast."

"I'll see how things go. I really need to get back in church though. All of my time have been consumed with homework and preparing assignments. I appreciate your support, Erica. Sometimes it's hard to figure things out on your own."

"Yes, it can be hard. Life is crazy, but we have to try to make the best of it."

"You're right. Don't be surprised if I ask you to celebrate with me again as I go through this journey. I'll try not to bug you too much though, but this is more challenging than I expected. I'll be fine, I just needed a change of environment."

"It's fine. I don't mind being your cheer leader. At times, we all need a little extra support," Erica said, smiling.

"We probably should head back home."

"Yeah, I told my hubby I wouldn't be gone too long."

"Plus, you two are newlyweds, so you can't be hanging out that much."

Erica chuckled. "That's true. I'm sorry things turned out the way they did Jazmine. But keep your head up."

"I will."

After paying the bill, they gave each other a hug, and said their goodbyes.

The next morning, after taking a much-needed jog, she took her puppy out for a short walk. Then began doing housework while listening to her Ledisi CD, and later called her mom.

"Hey Mom, how're you?"

"Hey Jazz, I'm doing good. I hope you haven't been studying too hard."

"Well, I try not to, but you know me. I have to squeeze it in between preparing assignments and grading homework. It's a challenge. But I'm doing alright. I received an "A" in both my classes, so I'm off to a good start."

"Good for you. You've always been determined to do your best. But you have to find time to have a little fun too."

"For sure. I went out to dinner with Erica last night, which was a nice break."

"Good. So, how're things with you and Noah? Are you two talking?"

"Yeah, we talk, and he's visited me a couple of times. And I have two dozen roses in my apartment."

"Oh wow. Well…"

"I don't know Mom. Erica mentioned maybe we should go to a marriage retreat. But I don't know much about how they work or if I want to even consider it."

"Do you still love him?"

"Huh?"

"Do you still love him, Jazmine?"

"I don't know. But what does that have to do with anything? It sure didn't seem to matter to him when he was in DC."

"I know honey. But things happen and since he's back home now, maybe y'all can work it out."

"Mom, you never would've put up with the things he's put me through. I mean, I bet dad never not returned your calls until the next day?"

"No, I never had that problem. But baby, you don't know everything me and your dad have gone through, and I don't want you to know either. Don't worry about what me or anyone else would put up with. Everyone has their own life to live, and we all have mess to deal with at different times in our lives. Trust me, we've had our struggles and almost said forget it, but we chose to stick it out and I'm glad we did. So, think about it and ask him about it if you think you might want to go that route. But it's all up to you Jazz. That's between you and him."

"Thanks mom. I didn't plan on discussing this with you, but I'm glad I did. I'll see how things go and I'll let you know. Thanksgiving is coming up soon, so I'll be there for dinner. I'll make a cake and a couple of sweet potato pies."

"That sounds good Jazz."

"And tell dad I said hi, and I'll talk with you again soon. Love you."

"I will. I love you too."

CHAPTER 29

A Surprise at Yoshi's

That afternoon, Noah called.

"Hey Jazz, how did your finals go?"

"They actually went well. I received an "A" in both classes."

"Good for you. But you're smart, so I'm not surprised. Do you feel up to celebrating your accomplishment? I realize you still have a long way to go, but we can celebrate as you go along."

"Um, yeah. Okay."

"Do you want me to come over or do you want to go out for dinner?"

"Let's go out."

"Would you like to go somewhere special?"

"I wonder if it's too late to get tickets for the show at Yoshi's. There is a jazz concert going on this weekend. We can have dinner than go to the show if it's not too late."

"I'll look into it, and I'll call you right back."

Ten minutes later, he called back.

"Hey Jazz, I got lucky, there were still tickets left."

"Perfect. I haven't been to a concert in a long time."

"I'll pick you up at 5:00, and we can have dinner there before the show starts."

"Alright, I'll see you at 5:00."

After dinner, they went into the concert venue for the Spyro Gyra show. Towards the middle of the concert, her stomach sank when she saw Marcus sitting at a table with another woman. She squinted her eyes while sipping her drink to make sure she wasn't mistaken. The woman had a striking appearance of sophistication. Jazmine smiled and grooved to the music, while trying not to show any reaction to seeing him enjoying his life with someone else. *Who in the hell is she? I mean, I know we're just friends, but I thought he wanted to be with me.*

"I love this music, they're so good," Noah said, while bobbing his head.

"Yes, they are. Um, I need to run to the lady's room for a quick minute. I'll be right back." *Why am I trippin'? They look so happy together. And here I am stuck with Mr. What's Next?* On the way back to her seat, she glanced over at them.

"Are you feeling alright?" Noah asked.

"Oh yeah, nature called."

Jazmine tried to enjoy herself but kept peeping over at Marcus. *Why is he touching her shoulder?* She became aware she had feelings for him and was confused on how to deal with it. When the lights came on during intermission, she remained seated with her back turned toward Marcus. During the last act she made up an excuse to leave before the show ended to avoid an encounter with him.

"Hey Noah, I'm kind of tired. Can we leave now?"

"Are you sure, it's almost over?"

"Yes, I'm sure."

"Okay," he said, placing her jacket over her shoulders. "I know you've had a lot on your plate since you've started school, so I'm sure you're tired."

"Yes, but I'll be fine. I just need to get some rest."

"This was just like old times when we use to go out to concerts," he said, walking to the car. "Did you enjoy the concert?"

"Yes, I did. But I know you love jazz music, so that was a real treat for you. I've never really been into jazz, but I really enjoyed myself."

Jazmine hoped he wouldn't expect her to invite him in when he took her home. She wasn't in the mood for company, especially seeing how Marcus had moved on with his life. When they got to her apartment, Noah walked in with her and sat on the couch. She went into her bedroom to change her shoes and hung up her jacket. *Why is he here, I should've told him not to come in.*

"Hey, do you feel better now that you're back home?"

"Yes, I do. I'm going to turn in shortly. Thank you for taking me out tonight. It was a lot of fun," she said, taking a bottled water from the fridge.

"I'm glad you enjoyed yourself. I had a good time being out with you tonight. Do you want to sit down and relax for a while?"

"No, I'm going to call it a night. I'll just talk with you tomorrow."

"Oh, are you asking me to leave?"

"Well, I'm tired Noah."

"But Jazmine…"

"Like you said I have a lot on my plate, so I need to get my rest."

"But I can sleep on the couch."

"Not this time Noah."

He shook his head in disbelief. She stood there gazing at him while waiting for him to stand up and leave.

"Jazmine, I don't understand why I can't stay. I mean...you are my wife."

"Noah please, don't even go down that road."

Jazmine needed to clear her mind, and she didn't want to pretend like everything was back to normal in their relationship. She needed space after seeing Marcus out on a date and she wasn't in the mood to be with Noah.

"Okay Jazz. I'll talk with you tomorrow."

"Alright, goodnight."

Sunday morning, she tuned in to watch the church service online. After having breakfast, she'd started grading her student's assignments. She picked up the phone a few times to call Marcus but kept changing her mind, then received a text from Erica.

Erica: Hey sis, how's it going? I was hoping I'd see you at service today.

Jazmine: I'm good, I didn't make it today. I watched it online. I decided to stay in and relax.

Erica: I hear you. It's important to get your rest. Okay, I was just checking on you. I'll be in touch.

Jazmine: Thanks for checking on me. I'll talk with you later.

Her phone rung before she could put it down. She figured Erica had forgotten to tell her something, until Marcus's name appeared on the caller ID.

"Hello?"

"Hey Jazmine, how're you?"

"Hey there, I'm good. How're you?"

"I'm good, missing you."

"Oh yeah." Jazmine smiled. "It's nice to hear from you."

"Do you feel like going out for dinner?"

"Sure."

"Cool, can I pick you up or would you prefer to meet at my place?"

"You can pick me up. My address is 6401-Shellmound Street, Apt. 206."

"Okay thanks. How does 6:00 sound?"

"Perfect."

"I'll see you then."

CHAPTER 30

After the Boat Cruise

Jazmine became nervous but excited to see Marcus. She wore her green off the shoulder pencil fitting dress, and green high heels. She appreciated having a new beginning and wanted to enjoy herself. She had plans to ask him about his personal life but wanted to wait until the right time. At 5:55, her doorbell rang.

"Uh oh, he's here," she said to herself. She looked through the peephole before opening the door.

"Hey Marcus, come on in," she said, giving him a quick hug.

"Hey there, don't you look beautiful. It's been a while since I've seen you."

"Thank you, Marcus. You look nice yourself."

"Your place is nice. I see you're good at decorating."

"Well, I try."

"I'm going to grab my jacket and purse. I'll be right back."

"Okay, I'll be here waiting."

She turned back and gazed at him and smiled. Marcus hadn't told her where they were going for dinner because he'd wanted to surprise her.

"I didn't expect this. This is really nice."

"I know. I've been wanting to take you out on a cruise for a while now. But you've been so busy, so I just waited until the right time."

While they had a drink, the band played a Luther Vandross tune.

"Would you like to dance? he asked"

"Yes, I would," she said, smiling.

She loved the special attention he gave her, and he held her close as they slow danced.

"Jazmine, I don't want this night to end," he whispered.

"Neither do I."

He stared into her eyes and gently rubbed her face with the back of his hand. "I really want to be with you Jazmine, but I don't want to rush you. I want things to be right. You're special to me and no matter what I will accept whatever you decide."

Her eyes were filled with tears, as she gazed into his. After the music ended, they'd held each other a bit longer before heading back to their seats. She picked up a napkin to dab her eyes as they sat down.

"I'm sorry Marcus. I just got a little overwhelmed."

"It's okay. I feel the same way."

After dinner, they danced again, and later stood on the deck and held hands while gazing at the stars. When the boat docked, they headed back to her apartment, when they'd found Noah standing outside of her door.

"There you are, I've been calling you," Noah said. "So, you were out on a date? Who is this?"

"Uh, what are you doing here?" Jazmine asked.

"Hey man what's up?" Noah said.

"Nothing man," Marcus replied.

"Noah, can you please leave?" Jazmine said.

"I'm not going anywhere. Now I see why you didn't answer your phone."

"My phone is on silent. Sounds familiar?" she said with a smirk on her face.

"Oh, so you're pulling one of those..."

"Excuse me." Jazmine stepped around him to unlock her door when Noah grabbed her arm.

"Hey man, get your hands off her," Marcus said.

Jazmine pulled her arm away from him. "Let me go Noah. Come on in Marcus," she said, opening her door.

Noah stepped in front of him. "Man, where're you going?"

Marcus pushed him back against the wall. "Man, get the hell back. You didn't take care of her when you had her, so get over it."

"Jazmine you're gonna pay for this," Noah said. "Then again, you ain't worth my time."

"Marcus, come in now," she said.

Jazmine closed the door, and left Noah standing outside.

"I don't want to leave you here alone. I don't feel comfortable knowing he might come back. Is it alright if I stay for a while?" Marcus asked.

"Yes, you can. I'm sorry about that."

Jazmine appreciated how Marcus stood up to Noah and loved how he wanted to protect her. They sat on the balcony and talked about how much they enjoyed the cruise, and how happy they were to finally get together again.

"Marcus, I have something to ask you. Are you seeing someone?"

"Uh, not seriously."

"Well. I was at Yoshi's last night and I saw you with someone. It looked serious to me."

"You were there?" He chuckled.

"Yes, I was."

"Why didn't you speak?"

"I don't know…I just didn't. So, who was she? I can tell she was someone special."

"Huh? Really."

"Don't play with me, Marcus."

"I'm not playing Jazmine. Are you jealous?"

"Just answer the question."

"You're jealous? I love it," he said, smiling.

"Forget it."

"Alright, alright, she was my younger sister. I took her out for her birthday. I reconnected with my family two weeks ago and I wanted to do something special for her. Gotcha," he said, smiling.

"Aww, that's so nice. You really did get me," she said, chuckling. "I'm so glad you reconnected with your family."

"Yes, it's been nice being around them. I never want to experience losing that connection with them again. So, how come you're just now telling me you saw us last night?"

"I don't know. I wasn't sure how to ask you about it."

He took her hand. "You can ask me anything at any time." He scooted his chair close to her and bent over and kissed her. "Jazmine, I want to be with you and only you. But I want you to feel the same way about me. I'll continue to be patient with you, but I need to know if you feel the same way about me."

"Yes...yes, I do, but I just need to handle this situation," she said, trying to hold back her tears. "And I can't start a relationship with you without setting some rules. For example, when I call you, you must answer or have a good reason why you didn't. You must consider my feelings at all times... you can't go away and not contact me for hours... and you can't take me for granted... and you must have a sense of humor, and—"

"Okay...okay, hold on a minute. I would never do those things to you. I'm not him, and I'm sorry you went through all of that. I want you to be my queen, I cherish you, Jazmine. Relax, and let's take one day at a time."

"I'm sorry, Marcus. I'm so used to fighting my way through to happiness."

"I understand, but you don't have to deal with that anymore. It's all over. I'm here now."

Jazmine wanted to accept what Marcus said, but she had reservations about how things would work out. She wanted to take her time and move slow in building their relationship. Her love for Noah had ceased and she needed to get rid of the baggage she'd been holding onto in dealing with him. She later filed for a divorce and continued her studies in psychology.

From then on, their relationship grew stronger, and he continued to support her desire to get her license. He showered her with love and affection and respected her in ways she'd never experienced before. She'd fallen in love with him and appreciated being cared for and loved without having to beg and plead for attention. Jazmine had now set her sights on another chance at love.

Made in the USA
Las Vegas, NV
17 October 2024

96981891R00121